The Soul Mate Search

By

Morgan K Wyatt

Published by The Sleeping Dragon Press

www.morgankwyatt.com
www.facebook.com/AuthorMorganKWyatt

Chapter One

NINA LOOKED AT the placard promising Tarot readings taped on the window of what appeared to be a junk store. The display crammed with decorative vases, statues of Greek Gods and Goddesses even had a few tribal masks that leered out at the passing crowd. It was the first time she'd noticed the small shop jammed between the carpet remnants store and yoga studio. Every other time she'd driven to the spice shop. Today she had walked since it was a gorgeous, sunny day. Besides, she could use the exercise. Tucking one finger into the waistband of her skirt, she tugged it outward to ease the bite. Her impulsive decision to go with a smaller size to encourage weight loss felt stupid and painful now.

Nonsense. That's what all card readings were. They were no more accurate than reading a fortune cookie and certainly no reason to waste good money to hear she had a handsome stranger in her future or that she couldn't decide between two men. Any real fortuneteller would know there were no men in her life. The lack was beginning to worry her, which was probably the reason she attacked every diet that came out. If only she'd dropped ten pounds, she'd be a knockout according to the gym trainer. Of course, he also wanted to sell a series of sessions to her there. It involved more free time than she had. Her best friend Ellie swore by the ginger regimen. The flavored water she tried at her friend's house didn't gag her too much, which was the reason she was off to buy an industrial size container of the stuff.

Two large steps took her past the lure of Tarot reading when an elderly woman appeared between the sliver of space between the buildings. She wore her hair in a chignon while her slender frame sported an elegant black dress. A few colorful necklaces hung from her neck while some sizable jewels glittered on her fingers. Her dark gaze met Nina's surprised one.

"You are leaving without even knowing the answer to your question."

Biting her lips, Nina debated what to say. At first, she wanted to deny having a question, but she did have one. If the woman knew she had a question, did that make her legitimate? It could be the fact she had hesitated in front of the store that had the woman hurrying out to drum up business. "Um…" What did one call a fortune teller?

The woman's eyes sparkled as if holding back laughter. "It's Helen, just Helen. I did not come out to drum up business." Her lips turned up into a smile at the phrase. "No, I came because I care about you."

Nina understood the retail business and *pretending to care* sold merchandise, but even knowing that the woman intrigued her. "Why do you care?"

Helen raised one delicately plucked eyebrow. "You are running out of time."

Nina automatically looked at her watch, wondering how late it was. What excuse could she use to get away from the woman? Weren't those who told your fortune for money supposed to say good things? How else would they get any repeat business? "I am in a bit of a rush."

"Perhaps that's your problem." Helen held up an admonishing finger and then added two more. "Three times you've passed your soul mate without giving him a glance. It is rare to have a soul mate, even rarer to have so many chances." Helen dropped her hand and contemplated her cuticles.

Soul mate, what soul mate? Somehow, she had passed the man. Trying to think of how many people she encountered every day working in at one of the biggest malls in the tristate region boggled her math ability. All the same, she had missed him three times. Three times? "How old was I when I missed him?"

Helen gestured to the shop door. "Perhaps you would like to keep your private life private."

Of course, she would. The idea of her missing *the one* had her demanding answers on a busy sidewalk. Who knows how many people overheard her? As the regional manager of men's suit and formal wear stores, she did have a business reputation to keep. When she took the management job ten years ago, constantly surrounded by men, Ellie had predicted wedding bells. In a way, she had the same thought, the reason she left managing a trio of candle shops.

She and Ellie failed to consider one thing. Most men who came to her shop for tuxedos or suits were getting married or very close to it. Often the fiancée managed the visit, which killed any chance of flirting if the men considered it. Still, she got a few dates from sales representatives who were trying to get her to pick up their line. Unfortunately, most of the dates were little more than sales pitches paired with wine and food.

Might as well listen to what the women had to say. It could be no worse than the ginger diet.

Helen skirted tables laden with curios and dust leading the way. After a long, twisted path, they reached a small room with a draped round table and two chairs, surprising her after the clutter of the outer room.

"Have a seat." Helen gestured to the chair, turning to remove something from a cabinet built into the wall.

Nina sat, perching on the edge, wondering if it was too late to leave. Helen turned and placed a white candle on the table along with a round glass sphere. It was an honest to goodness crystal ball. Leaning closer, Nina examined the object. Only a little bigger than a softball, instead of being clear, it had a whitish, frosted aspect to it. She wondered how anyone could see anything in it. A cynic would reason that was the idea. Helen walked around the table, making Nina wonder what she was doing. Every time she passed behind her, Nina twisted in her chair to keep her in view. She didn't expect the woman to attack her, but crazier things happen. Less than a month ago, a little old lady with a butcher knife mugged her friend in the hospital parking lot.

"Rest easy, Nina. This is a safe place. You are safe." Helen made her third turn around the table and slipped into her chair. Pulling out a box of matches, she lit one and held it to the wick of the white candle until it caught.

No cards on the table. How would she do a reading? Nina was about to point this out when Helen spoke.

"Pick up the sphere and hold it. Consider your questions. Close your eyes."

She reached for the ball, vowing not to close her eyes. She rolled the ball between her fingers feeling the smooth glass. The frosted inside began to look cloudier. Indistinct shapes moved inside the glass and took form. The outline of her old elementary school solidified as she held the ball closer with the image of her mother walking her to school.

She twisted and danced at the end of her mother's hand, convinced she did not need parental supervision to walk the two blocks to school. Her mother determinedly held on, believing otherwise. The school buses roared up to the school, ejecting their load of noisy children.

One dark haired boy with a superhero backpack ran up the school stairs, turned, stopped, and looked back at her. Their eyes met for the briefest second.

His red polo and jeans could belong to any other male student, but she knew in an instant that it was him, her soul mate. She held the globe at eye level to get a closer look. No doubt, the man had changed in thirty years, but something might remain to help her find him. A name on a folder or some identifying mark on his clothing, there had to be something.

The crystal, instead of cooperating, grew foggy again. A sudden urge to pitch the faulty ball swept over her, but her hands remained locked in position. Her gaze went to Helen's, curious if she had something to do with the ball remaining stationary as opposed to airborne.

"Crystal balls are expensive." She winked, confirming her mental hold on Nina's throwing arm. "Look quickly or you will miss your second meeting."

The ball fogged and shifted once more when another image formed.

Her small car was loaded down with all she thought essential for college life, including twenty pairs of shoes, her laptop, no less than 200 romantic comedies DVDs, and enough toiletries and makeup to do one floor of her dorm. She struggled with a large box she had over-packed. A masculine voice broke into her struggles.

"Could you use some help?"

She gave up her box with a sigh of relief and recited her room number. She watched the box walk away with the assistance of two jean clad legs and athletic shoes. She didn't even see his face. He left the carton in front of her door, never giving her the chance to thank him. She never knew who carried her box. Her intentions were to make him cupcakes, which were difficult with the dorm's limited kitchen facilities, but even harder since she didn't know his name.

She watched him walk away in the globe, admiring how well he filled out his jeans. One of her girlfriends bragged how she could identify any man by looking at his backside. She could recognize him walking away, but it would make her no better than the men who always looked at her breasts and never quite made it up to her face. She wanted to whine but felt the psychic's grip over her hands. "I wasn't going to throw it this time."

"I can feel your frustration." Helen nodded as if agreeing with herself.

Exhaling deeply, Nina rolled her shoulders while keeping a firm grip on the ball. "How would you feel if you discovered you went to the same grade school as your soul mate, even the same college? Yet, you both managed to pass each other."

Helen smiled wistfully as if contemplating a memory Nina couldn't see. "I would feel very, very blessed. You aren't always reunited with your soul mate in each lifetime. It is such a grand experience. The euphoria lingers into the next life." The rapturous look on her face faded, confirming the suspicion that Helen's soul mate had not appeared in this lifetime.

"Oh." Nina grasped for something better, but came up with nothing. The ball started to heat under her hands as if responding to her emotional state. The McMillan and Sons building materialized in the glass.

Her first job after college, but already she'd given her notice, anxious for a chance to prove her worth at Candle World. However, before she could start her new adventure, Mr. McMillan gave her the odd job of hiring her own replacement. She shuffled through the resumes putting them in the order the interviews would be.

Antonius Dunn was last out of five candidates. The first name sounded foreign, but she noticed they graduated from the same college, which caused her to discount his first name. By interview number three, Mr. McMillan informed her that Joseph, nephew of the owner, had the job. Joseph wasn't well qualified, but Mr. McMillan made it known he wanted Joseph. The interviews and the ad in the paper were all a smokescreen to hide a clear case of nepotism. It didn't seem fair to interview the other candidates, leading them on with the possibility of being hired. She walked into the company lobby where the last two candidates waited, a well-groomed blonde woman with an air of superiority and a gorgeous, be still my heart, man.

Ah yes, she remembered now. She could hardly bring herself to look at the two of them since she was the bearer of bad tidings. The woman didn't matter too much because she had the look. Daddy could pull a few strings and get her a much better job than this. The man she remembered. Just one look at him and her heart stumbled. If she ever designed her ideal man, it'd be him. His dark curly hair skimmed his shoulders with the emphasis on artist as opposed to MBA. He had a pair of trendy wireless glasses and deep brown eyes. How she noticed so much at the time, it took her to say, "The position has been filled. Thanks for coming," amazed her.

The woman left in a huff, while he stood, towering over her a few inches. He held out his hand, and she touched it hesitantly, knowing touching it would be electrifying. It was. He thanked her for her time, repeated his name and left. She stood there with her hand out as if turned into a statue. Peggy, the receptionist, broke into her stupor. "That one was a looker. I would rather have him around than dumpy old Joseph."

Nina stared into the crystal ball at her younger self, transfixed by the closed door. She didn't need to remember what she was thinking then. Any woman-would wish Antonius would come back. Helen cleared her throat, catching her attention.

"Helen, the gorgeous guy is my soul mate? I don't get it. Men who look like him don't go for me. I'm average, a sparrow while he's a hawk. If I remember correctly, hawks eat sparrows." Her hands still clutched the ball as if she could bring back the image.

The woman's laughter tinkled and shimmered like wind chimes. "My girl, you have to see past the outside trappings into the man within. You two are destined to be together."

This sounded great in theory. "How do I meet my soul mate? Will he know I am his soul mate? I know his name, and he's probably in the area. All I have to do is look him up, right?"

The woman's forehead beetled as she chewed her bottom lip, not a good sign. Holding her hand out for the crystal ball, Helen took it and returned it to the cabinet. With her back turned, she started talking, making it hard to hear her clearly.

"It won't be easy. Your last meeting was almost thirteen years ago. Things change. People change. Antonius could have married."

"What?" Nina shot to her feet. "First, you tell me I have a soul mate and I need to find him because time is running out, then you say he might be married. Why?" Her fingertips gripped the table.

Putting her hands together in front of her chest, Helen waited, probably for Nina to appear less hostile. Realizing the elderly woman might view her as threatening, she sat and loosened her grip on the table. Her hand went up to her neck, which felt a little heated. Turning forty stalked her the way a cat did a bird. She'd given up any hope of having children and a husband too. Now she finds out her soul mate existed mere miles, possibly blocks from her. Instead of watching endless romantic movies, she could have been starring in her own.

Wait, she could have gone to her prom with Antonius, instead of Ellie's brother. The name was a mouthful. She could call him Anton. No, it didn't sound right. Tony seemed better.

Helen held out her hand as if pleading for her understanding. "Some things I know. Others I don't. You walk pass the store and your thoughts shout '*Where's my soul mate?*'"

Nina's eyes narrowed. She didn't like the image of her thoughts shouting. It made her sound pathetic. "My thoughts didn't yell."

"They did." Helen disagreed. "That's why I had to come out of the shop to quiet them down. I had no clue how long you and your screaming thoughts would be in the area."

"Now, they're screaming thoughts." This was not helping in the least. "Tell me about my soul mate and how I am running out of time."

Helen sat down, spreading her long fingers out on the table, showing off her rings. Nina noticed none was a wedding ring.

"That's right, no soul mate for me in this lifetime. My gift allowed me to see this so I did not hope for one. You have had more chances than most. Chances come in magical denominations. Three is one magical grouping, but lucky for you, three isn't it. You have four more chances."

Four more chances sounded as if a multitude. Surely, with four chances she could make it work. She'd always managed to get what she set her mind to, including her MBA, her home, and her current job. Why not Tony? "Is Tony looking for his soul mate?"

"I can't tell you. He may think he's already found his soul mate. He may be married." She shrugged her thin shoulders.

Not what she wanted to hear. "Please stop. Such possibilities are no help to me at all. What am I supposed to do with a man who is married?" She didn't consider herself a femme fatale who would cause a man to abandon his wife and family. Her Nona would be appalled at such behavior. It turned her stomach too. Who knew finding a soul mate would be so frigging hard.

Helen stretched across the table to pat Nina's hand. "Don't fret too much. Even if he's married, I doubt it will last long. Marriages seldom do these days. Besides, you can't force the meetings. They just happen when everything falls into place."

Her plan to search the Internet using the services she used for employee background checks skidded to an abrupt halt. "I can't do what?" Her other plans, where she'd get the works, complete with eyebrows and other areas waxed, ended up on temporary hold also.

"No, you cannot mess with fate. She can be a cruel bitch. Consider you know more than most people do in your position. You've seen your other half. You even know his name. All you have to do is be aware, ready, for the next chance." Helen gave her hand a squeeze before letting go and standing.

It didn't take a rocket scientist to recognize the signal for the reading was over. Standing, she grabbed her purse and rifled through the wallet, thinking she should give the woman something. "How much do you usually charge for a reading?"

Her fingers rested on a twenty as Helen said, "Sixty-five."

The twenty would make a decent tip. You'd think if she charged so much the place would look better.

Helen laughed again, motioning her through the store. "It wouldn't do me any good to look too prosperous in this neighborhood. An update on how your soul mate search concludes will be my payment."

The door closed behind her. Standing on the sidewalk, Nina stared at the people walking around her. She needed to be on full alert. She would never know when Antonius might show up. With that in mind, she headed for the spice shop. No time like the present to drop the ten pounds settled around her torso.

By the time she returned to her office one of the sales rep from the Allegro line had left a pound of free trade Sumatran coffee. The bag rattled when she shook it, indicating beans. No good. Her grinder broke a couple of weeks ago, probably due to overwork. A good cup of coffee sounded like heaven. Sighing, she pushed the bag aside and paged through the suit catalog that accompanied the beans.

Most people believe when you advertised custom suits they are designed for each individual, which was not the case. They had to start somewhere. Usually, her tailors had a series of suits they adapted to fit each client. They did an excellent job, often making the customer better dressed than most millionaires. The Allegro line catalog featured glossy page after glossy page of lean, sexy models, wearing light colored suits. Sometimes the suits were even unconstructed. Her clients preferred padding. The more padding in the shoulders, the better the waist looked.

Allegro. She considered the word, rolling it around in her mouth. It reminded her of allergy medicine. It was hard to sell a suit with a similar name to allergy medicine. Too bad, she pushed the catalog away. Some of the suits had potential, especially if she wanted to appeal to a younger set. They could bypass mentioning the name. Up to now, she hadn't even met the Allegro rep. He always dropped in when she was gone. Of course, the rep could be a woman too. She picked up the scrawled note that came with the coffee.

To N. M. Bradley,

Enjoy the coffee and the catalog. Both pack robust charm and character, which should 'suit' your discerning taste.

T. Dante

The note told her exactly nothing. It was an amusing note and approach, similar to something she might have written. The digital clock glowed five-fifteen, which mean most of her junior executives had left the building, pleading t-ball games, scouts, and dance lessons for their little princes or princesses. She didn't begrudge them family time, but she often wondered how much of it was actually t-ball lessons or wind-down time at the local sports bar around the corner.

The few times she decided to nip out for a bite at Sammy's Bar and Grill, she found a handful of her employees who quickly muttered various excuses for their early departure. The place's reputation was for their breaded tenderloin and scantily clad waitresses. Sometimes it embarrassed her to stop in for a burger, but not as much as it should embarrass Hector, who claimed to leave early on Wednesdays for prayer meeting. Did they lie to her face about their plans because she was female? It really didn't matter since she mentally noted who kept showing up at the sports bar. A smart man would know enough to go somewhere else once caught by the boss. Apparently, she had a few who weren't too sharp.

Her female employees actually did manage to make it home, fix dinner, and help with homework as they said they were. If not, she never caught them at Sammy's or in the mall as she walked to the parking lot. Since she had no home life per se, she stayed late. Ellie, her best friend, pointed out she had no social life because she spent most of her waking hours at her job. It was rather a Catch-22 situation. She could have married, was even asked twice, but it didn't feel right.

She expected something more than the routine proposals she received. The men who rendered the proposals were good, decent men, as her mother liked to remind her. Now they were married with children. Her mother always tacked on the additional info, in case she'd somehow forgotten. Sometimes she saw them in town, often with the family in tow. At best, she nodded when she saw them, aware a wife would not appreciate an enthusiastic greeting. Often, she watched them before they saw her, trying to decide if the men looked happy. For the most part, they looked harried and tired. Still, they were probably happier without her by their side.

Neither Tim nor Paul had confessed to great passion in their proposals. Nope, it was more like if you don't have any plans for the rest of our life, then why don't we marry. She wondered if they ran the same proposal past their current wives. If they did, apparently the women weren't doing anything with the rest of their lives. They could have fallen madly, passionately in love. Thinking of the two earnest men, she snorted with laughter, glanced at her door to see it was open. It wasn't.

The clock now glowed five-thirty-one. She might as well head home and start her ginger diet. Tucking the coffee under her arm, she prepared to leave. Glancing in the mirror on her office wall, she reapplied her lipstick and corralled some wayward strands of hair back in her French twist hairstyle. The small twelve inch by twelve inch mirror reflected a woman in a dark suit with a bright fuchsia silk blouse. Her makeup and hair reflected her place on the corporate ladder. Her index finger smoothed her foundation. When it came to makeup, she was her own worst enemy, often scratching her face or rubbing her eyes. Well, she was good to go now.

Striding through the showroom, she called out goodbyes to the remaining associates. A client came out of the dressing room, looking unsure in their top of the line suit. The slightly pudgy man was not the type to attract women's eyes, she knew. Feeling playful, she eyed him, before whistling, and calling out, "Looking good."

No doubt, the man regarded her curiously along with her three sales reps. She was out to find her true love. It was about time too. She walked with a bit of a bounce in her step, watching the reflective store windows for a sign of Mr. Wonderful. Nothing yet. At least she had her coffee. Bending her head slightly, she inhaled the heavenly aroma.

Chapter Two

SHE MADE IT all the way to her car with no soul mate in sight. How disappointing, but the day wasn't over. Nina wasn't sure how the man would get to her house unless he were a delivery guy or a burglar. She had no plans to eat out. Could be today wasn't her day to meet him. Inside her car, she hooked her phone up to the USB dock so she could talk hands-free, which was another good thing about being on her own. No way could she hold a conversation with a van full of children.

Ellie answered on the first ring as if expecting her. "Hello, Cinder-Ellie," Nina teased, resorting to her childhood nickname. It was no favorite of her friend, created by some jerky sixth-grade cheerleader. Ellie might remember Antonius from school.

"Hello yourself, Nina Nano," her friend teased back. The same cheerleader had kept rather busy, renaming all the students. Because she was part of the cool kids group, everyone assumed it was equally cool to sport the nicknames proudly. Nina knew enough not to use hers and discouraged anyone who tried to, except Ellie.

"Ellie, I was wondering if you remember a boy named Antonius Dunn in first grade?" There was silence on the other end of the line. "Ellie?"

"I'm thinking. We're talking thirty-three years. I do good to remember my own name. What did he look like?"

"Average kid with brown eyes and hair. He grew into a gorgeous man, though." Her voice warmed, reliving the moment when he touched her hand.

"This sounds interesting. Did you see him today?" Her friend asked as Nina eased into traffic.

"In a way," she hedged. "The actual meeting was thirteen years ago."

"What? Did I hear you right?" Disbelief colored her friend's word. The side lane faded away as Nina moved her expensive sedan into the appropriate lane. She watched the diminishing road carefully. Here it comes, the idiot of the day. A minivan careened into her lane almost clipping her. Her hand went for the horn without thinking. The kid in the back seat gave her the finger, causing her to hit her horn again. She wanted one of those. Her children would behave like humans as opposed to thugs in training.

"Having trouble on the vanishing lane road again?" her friend inquired, knowing the answer.

Still angry, she gave the horn another push. It didn't solve anything. It vented some anger, but that was all. There was a good chance tomorrow the same woman would cut her off again. She wondered if the van driver somehow knew she hugged the shoulder to keep from getting her expensive car nicked. Somehow, they'd justify their behavior while claiming she was the problem. She lived the life she ended up with, but was it the life she wanted?

"Yes, I'm not sure why every other person is convinced it's their right to disregard all the right lane ending signs and cut someone off because of their failure to think. Ironically, the person who rear-ends them is at fault."

She growled the last words, thankful for her superior brakes, which kept her from hitting anyone. Her luxury sedan wasn't what she really wanted, but somehow she talked herself out of the fire engine red convertible. She didn't think it was suitable for her position. She doubted the thought would even cross a man's mind. She'd take a hit on the resale value since the car was so new if she traded it in, but she deserved to get what she wanted.

"Where did you see your gorgeous man today?" Ellie's voice came over the car speakers, filling the acoustically perfect interior.

The sound system was a feature she did enjoy. It certainly made listening to music a pleasure. Caught up in the pros and cons of her vehicle, she answered without thinking. "In a crystal ball."

Ellie's laughter sank into the padded interior. "That's rich. You had me going there for a while."

"No, I am serious. I met a fortune teller today, Helen, who told me Antonius is my soul mate. I've met him three times so far. I only have four times left to get it right. I need to be serious about this if I don't want to die a lonely old woman surrounded by cats. They'll end up feasting on my dead body." The image made her shiver.

The elaborate brick walls and iron wrought gates of her neighborhood came into view. She brought the sedan to a stop to type in her passcode. The gates swung open as she thumbed in the last number. She drove through the gates watching in her rearview mirror for anyone trying to run through on her code. What was the point of a gated neighborhood, if it didn't keep her safe? Elaborate brick homes with minuscule yards lined the road. Her home was tiny at only two thousand square feet, but she lived alone. How much space did she truly need?

Ellie continued to chatter. "Nina, you don't have any cats. You hate cats."

"Of course, I don't. It is obvious they eat the owners once they die. It's a good reason not to have one." Her garage door opened as it sensed the car's approach. Thank goodness for smart houses. It was a blessing most of the time. Except when a computer glitch locked her out of her house for a day until they could get it fixed. The neighborhood wasn't where she really wanted to live, either. Her secret dream was to live near the water, possibly even a houseboat. Only the truly eccentric lived on boats or people who couldn't afford houses in gated neighborhoods.

"El, I am going to unhook you for a second to go in the house."

Her actions suited her words as she put the phone up to her ear. Twenty minutes later, her friend had talked her down from her soul mate high. There wasn't a wonderful man out there waiting for her, just a handful of mediocre men other women rejected. Nina was currently working her way through those men via online dating.

If a little ginger stimulated your system, then a lot was bound to help. She quadrupled the amount and chugged it down. The spice burned, and the water didn't seem to relieve her thirst, either. Another glass didn't help. Oh well, she'd work out on her treadmill and then nuke dinner.

Changing into a faded pair of shorts and a T-shirt, she headed for the treadmill. Living alone and having no social life meant she could leave the treadmill in the living room to watch her television shows on the wide screen while exercising. An exciting chase resulted in her pushing up the speed and elevating her heartbeat. Sometimes a love scene elicited the same reaction.

Nina mentally went through her to-do list as she jogged. Damn, she forgot to drop by the store and get her coffee ground. Eventually, the grinder she ordered online would arrive, but not by tomorrow. She wasn't out of coffee, but if she didn't do it tonight, she'd forget, ending up out of coffee. It was the reason she brought the coffee home, and the fact it smelled delicious. Besides, if she left it at the office, there would be an unspoken obligation to share. Her excellent bribe coffee would be gone in less than a day. At home, it might last a week or more. Grocery store trip tonight, not her favorite idea, but she didn't see any way around it.

The scenes of her favorite television drama blared in the background as she tried to recall the youngish Antonius. He'd changed some, but probably not too much. People told her she looked the same as she did in college, which she assumed was a compliment. It could have been a backhand slam, implying a lack of sophistication.

Her stomach gurgled ominously, not the usual I-am-hungry-feed-me sounds, but rather the I-am-going-to-be-sick noise. Punching the speed button, she slowed down to a fast walk. No time to be sick. Worse yet, there wasn't anyone to replace her if she was ill. In theory, she should have a right-hand person, but that would mean giving up some of her control. If she was nothing else, she was a control freak, which explained her five and ten-year plans. Taking no time for illness, she generally went to work with a box of tissues and cough drops. Being the top dog allowed her to have her own bathroom, which helped when she was gut-wrenching sick.

Her skin felt hot and itchy. She rubbed a hand over her feverish face. The heat might be due to the running or thoughts about her hunky soul mate. She knew better. Damn, she didn't need this. Her stomach gave another threatening growl. Stopping the treadmill, she decided to make an immediate run to the store, and then off to bed. Two PM pain relievers should send her into a deep slumber. There were few things drugged sleep couldn't cure. A raging libido was one of them at least she'd rest.

A quick glance in the hall mirror revealed a ratty ponytail, her faded 5k shirt, and equally shabby shorts. It would need to be a quick trip. No one would see her. Changing her clothes would take time she didn't have from the sounds her body was emitting. Some ginger ale would help her rebelling stomach. Grabbing her coffee, she headed for the garage.

On the way to the store, she cataloged her symptoms. Sweating would indicate a fever, wouldn't it? Her uneasy stomach might signify food poisoning. What did she eat? She ended up skipping lunch from spending too much time with the fortune teller. Her head hurt, but it could be from staring at the computer screen too long. It could be allergies. Her skin felt itching, tingling. She shifted in her seat, aware her over-sensitized skin extended below the waistline. Not a symptom of any illness, she could remember. Sighing, the image of her shaking hands with Antonius came to mind and the jolt of electricity *or was it chemistry*, she'd felt.

Oh well, she'd need to forget all about that. Ellie managed to convince her it was a fraud. Still, she had held the globe in her hands, those were her memories, and not a dollar had exchanged hands. Still, it might be a come-on to get her to return and lay down good money to find out more about her soul mate. Helen had emphasized she couldn't force a meeting. It could be if she met her soul mate on her own, she wouldn't need the services of a fortune teller, especially a cryptic one.

Rain started by the time she pulled into the grocery store parking lot. Her planned sprint turned into a walk as dizziness swept over her. Great, all she needed was to pass out. Making it into the store foyer, she shook, to rid herself of the excess moisture no doubt resembling a dog. The store cranked up the air conditioning frequently, but today with damp clothing, it was frigid.

She rushed through the shop as her arms goose-pimpled from the chill. A quick glance down at her wet shirt explained why the man stocking sodas stared at her, well at her chest anyhow. Pulling the wet shirt away from her skin, she headed for the grinder. Pouring the coffee beans into the grinder, she mentally calculated how long it would take her to return to the sanctuary of her house. So far, so good, no one she knew had seen her. Just as well, she didn't want to make polite with anyone. Her bed called out to her. She could hear its siren call over the sound of the coffee grinder.

Inhaling the aroma of fresh ground beans, deeply, she thought the heavenly scent by itself might heal her. Taking her coffee, ginger ale, and snatching up some yogurt, she headed for the self-check scanner. She was ready to explain to the cashier who monitored the aisles, she'd brought the coffee in with her, but the woman never looked up from her perusal of a gossip magazine.

Her purchases bagged, she headed for the car. All she had to do was reach her car without any human interaction, when a man, walking in, spoke to her.

"Your coffee smells wonderful. Is it a Sumatran blend?"

She looked up into the face of a smiling man with curling damp hair and water spotted glasses. Her brain went dead. The absolute worst time to meet anyone, she managed to mumble her reply. "I think it is." She walked away, hoping he wasn't watching her. Why couldn't she run into men like that when she was dressed for work?

Unlocking her car, she slipped on the smooth leather seat since her legs were wet. Could she look any worse? Men didn't typically try to strike up conversations with her in the grocery store, except the butcher who cajoled her into buying a more expensive cut of meat. Twisting the key in the ignition, she headed for home. The brief flash of the man who talked to her came to mind. He was taller than she was, a little on the lanky side, curly hair with a few threads of silver, glasses, and brown eyes. Her foot stomped on the brakes. Oh my God, it was her soul mate!

She'd just botched Meeting Number Four. He was actually trying to be friendly, and she all but ran away from him. This could be the reason she was single. She folded under flirtation. Turning her music down, she called Ellie by using the controls on the steering wheel.

"Ellie, I saw him. Meeting Number Four. I botched it because I was feeling so funny, all itchy and hot. Even my stomach wasn't cooperating."

She waited for her friend to exclaim over the possibility of meeting her soul mate.

"Nina, how much ginger did you ingest?"

Why did she want to know that? When she had just seen the man of her happily ever after? He acted interested in her, even though she was wearing her faded wet clothes. Were her nipples standing at attention? That might explain it. "Oh, I don't know. Lots, I wanted to get the weight loss started."

"It might explain your stomach issues. I'm not sure about the other things. I did read that too much ginger could stimulate arousal in women. I'm not sure if it's true or not."

"Trust me, it wasn't the ginger. It was all pure, delicious male."

Ellie's sign of exasperation came over the phone line. "Girl, you need to get out, preferably get laid. What about your date with the magazine photographer? What was his name?"

"Gavin." She didn't want to talk about Gavin. He was a perfectly fine man, but he didn't strike any sparks.

"Give Gavin a try. Didn't he want to go out with you again?"

"Yes." She knew what Ellie was doing, being sensible, steering her away from her fantasy man.

Her friend had a point. After all, she appeared content with her sweetie, even though Nina found Justin way too arrogant for her taste. Besides, he never took Ellie anywhere, which often made her wonder if he was married or just thoughtless.

The excitement of realizing she may have talked to her soul mate fizzled away. Whom was she kidding? Nope, she was not the type to star in a romance novel. Why did she keep forgetting that? Extraordinary things do not happen to ordinary people. She'd give Gavin a call. No doubt, he'd turn her down, miffed she didn't accept a follow-up date. How could she get him to go out with her? Had it come down to this, trying to entice a man she didn't especially care for to go out with her?

TONY WALKED INTO the kitchen, placed his groceries down on the counter with a grimace. "I'm back with supper fixings."

Daniel wandered in from the hall with a slightly sleepy look on his face. "You back already? I napped a bit. Pick up any hot babes on your grub run?"

Reading the pizza box, Tony programmed the stove. "Actually," he said without turning away from the stove, "I saw one attractive woman. She had a damp, rumpled look as if she just rolled out of bed after a marathon lovemaking session. She had gorgeous long legs. Her wet shirt clung to her breasts, either she was cold or very excited to see me."

His lips curved up in memory. Something about her stuck with him. Had he seen her somewhere before?

Daniel opened the fridge to grab a beer and then boosted himself up on the counter to continue his conversation. "Did you make your play? Get her digits?"

"Nope." Tony slid the frozen pizza into the oven. Turning, he rested back against the corner. "I asked about the coffee she was carrying, and she practically ran away from me. I did get an excellent view of her rounded backside as she darted across the parking lot."

Taking a swig of his brew, Daniel swallowed and shook his head. "You have lost your touch. Too long out of the dating game. Sheila broke you good."

Tony's nostrils flared a little as he tried to control an upsurge of anger. He wasn't so much mad at Daniel for stating the obvious, but more at himself. "You're right. I should have been suspicious of the one woman who didn't want to get married. She threw me out of my house when she found someone new."

Daniel shook his bottle to check the level. "I don't mind you crashing with me and all, but why did you leave?"

"Surprise mainly. I come back early from a business trip to find Sheila in bed with a neighbor. It made me wonder if she made a habit of frequenting the neighbor men. My intention wasn't to leave permanently, but to walk off my anger. The few hours I was gone, she had the locks changed on the house. Now, it is up to my lawyer to get me back into my house." He pushed away from the counter to grab a beer too.

Daniel whistled. "I always considered her a piece of work after she came on to me at your holiday party."

Slamming his just-opened beer on the counter, he sloshed some onto his hand. "What? You never told me?"

"Hey, no reason for me mentioning it if the two of you were happy."

Tony picked up his beer and drained half of it before speaking. "Trust me, we weren't happy. I could never fully relax with her. She was always holding back on me. It never occurred to me she was holding back on the number of men she was currently sleeping with. I am a lousy judge of women."

"One woman. That's all. We all make mistakes. Remember Ronya? I moved across the country only to end up dumped her two months later. Tell me more about your luscious grocery woman." Daniel wiggled his eyebrows.

"Oh yeah, she was hot for me. Crazy about me. I had to peel her off it was so embarrassing. No way, I'll see her again. If I did, she'd probably run away from me again. I must have *damaged* tattooed on my forehead." He pushed up his hair, exposing a clear forehead with only a few light lines running across it.

"Don't see anything," Daniel reassured him, before pawing through the grocery sack, pulling out milk, eggs, cheese, and butter.

Picking up the perishables, Tony placed them in the fridge. Task completed, he faced his friend. "You are not supposed to see it. It is a message for other women, not you."

Sucking in his lips, Daniel considered the words. "Who wrote this invisible message?"

Finishing his beer in a long gulp, he sat down the bottle. "It's obvious. Sheila wrote it. She wants to warn other women about what a loser I am. Beware! Don't waste your time."

Daniel pretended to gag, slapping his chest. "Cut the maudlin self-pity. You are a great guy. If you weren't my friend, I wouldn't be able to stand you. When you're around, the women eyeball you while managing to look through me. You got an abstracted artist look. As for being a loser, you are an award-winning salesperson. In the land of casual Fridays you manage to sell millions of suits."

Women stared at him instead of Daniel. He found it hard to believe, especially when Daniel resembled a famous blond actor. Half the time people thought he was the actor, trying to go incognito. He rubbed his hand over his face to hide his smile. He liked the idea of women staring at him, even though Daniel made up crap to make him feel better about throwing away two years of his life on Sheila. Now, he couldn't even remember why he did it. They were more like roommates who sometimes slept together. If his life wasn't sucky enough, he kept on missing a potential contact, Bradley, the one big deal he needed to land. If he didn't know better, he'd think the man was avoiding him.

"I'm not so sure I'll be salesman of the year this year. I am having some trouble landing a major account. As for women looking at me, they do, but they are probably not thinking how much they want me.

Trust me. I have not been fending off women. Maybe I should take a pass on dating at least until I figure out why I always attract the wrong type." The thought depressed him. He'd taken no joy in signing the paperwork to evict Sheila from his house. No doubt, the conniving bitch would pick him clean or at least damage the house on her way out. It would be hard living there with the memories. The best he could do was sell it.

"You are off your game. That's normal. I am going to a concert this weekend. Why don't you come along? I see you aren't taking my advice. The best way to get over an old girlfriend is to get on top of a new one. You might as well get out and be seen."

Really? His friend was so sexist, and yet he did land the females at least for a short time, which might be all Tony wanted. Truthfully, he needed to get back into his house. Staying there was cramping Daniel's action. A concert might be fun. Drink a few beers, sing along with the artists, and forget for a moment that he was the owner of a broken life. "Sure, why not?"

"Great, I need to call Deidre and tell her she's been replaced." Daniel scooted off the counter to search for his cell phone.

"Wait. Don't do that. She'll be upset, and she might not ever go out with you again." Tony protested, following his friend.

"No problem, remember bro before—"

"Stop, don't say it. I prefer not to think of women that way. Why would you ditch this woman?"

Daniel stopped walking. His face expressed his confusion. "It's no big deal. I was going to dump her anyhow. There's no challenge to her, no chase. She's gotten to the point where she wants a relation-ship."

"Aren't you afraid of running out of women and being..." his friend was already out of listening range, "...alone," He said the word, knowing he was expressing his fears, not Daniel's.

He was alone. The oven timer buzzed, but food no longer exerted its usual siren song. All the same, he needed to get the pizza out before it burned. Using the pizza box as a base, he slid the hot pizza onto it, thinking about Sheila. He couldn't call her the love of his life. He hadn't had one yet. Maybe he never would. All the love nonsense was to sell stuff to women. Somehow, it sucked him in too. Using the pizza cutter, he sliced the pizza into eight relatively equal slices.

"Dinner," he called. He slid one piece onto a plate. Not eating would cause Daniel to make some remark about a pity party or remind him of Sheila. Besides, he'd had doubts for a year or more. He quit putting money into their joint account, and Sheila said nothing. Anything he valued from his autographed books to his golf clubs, he kept in his car. His actions probably said more than hers did. He was living with a woman he didn't trust, never mind love.

Chapter Three

GAVIN SOUNDED SO pleased when she called, Nina felt a bit like a puppy kicker. Kick the man and he still came back panting, eager for more. The man was presentable in his khakis and polo shirt. As a photographer for a world-renown magazine, he had the same issues she did, meeting someone while married to your work. He traveled the world as opposed to visiting the states, as she did.

His hand on her shoulder guided her to their concert seats, which were good ones. He offered her the aisle seat while taking the one, putting him next to a stranger. Since what kind of person it would be was always a tossup at a concert, she appreciated his thoughtfulness. You could get someone who always stomped on your toes in the process of leaving or a boozy want-to-be artist who sang along with every song, inventing words he couldn't remember. Last time, she had the privilege of a husband and wife behind her, arguing through the entire concert. She couldn't understand why they didn't fight at home, instead of sharing it with the crowd.

Gavin and she chattered a little bit about his recent trips. Technically, this was their second date, meaning she didn't know a lot about him. Was he divorced? No wife would tolerate his globetrotting ways, even if it were his job. Did she want to be in a relationship where the man was gone seventy-five percent of the time? What was she doing, making excuses for not seeing him again before he'd stated any intentions to do so?

Gavin turned and smiled at her. "I've been watching the crowd. There isn't another lady as beautiful and classy as you are."

"Thank you," she replied, wondering if she should mention his attempt at flattery inferred he'd been staring at other women and comparing them to her. Gavin, despite all his international assignments, retained an air of naiveté. She knew he meant it to be a compliment. It was fitting since she donned a colorful dress with a cutaway back, perfect for a summer concert. Her hair's side pony minimized the damage the humidity would do. Overall, she looked good. The dress emphasized her breasts and downplayed her waist.

Gavin offered to get her a drink. Various stands littered the edges of the concert area promising beer, buckets of rum punch, and drinks referred to as Slammers. She probably should bypass alcohol since Ellie felt she was getting desperate in the sexual needs department. No telling what she might do to the poor man. Gavin struck her as the—if he did the deed—it would be equivalent to a proposal. Her eyes roamed the aisles, looking for a regular soda vendor when she saw him.

His hair was beautifully styled with tiny threads of silver showing in the dark. He had on an ironed long sleeved, striped Oxford shirt, turned up cuffs. The same brown eyes framed by the familiar glasses. Then there was his long-legged stride, reminding her of a big cat stalking his prey, except he wasn't stalking his prey or was he? As he came closer, he looked right at her and winked. *He winked.* She couldn't believe it. Was her mouth open?

Gavin leaned over, interrupting the tiny moment of contact. "Did you want a regular cola or diet?"

"Diet." The words left her mouth without any thought, her mind on her soul mate. He was here. She couldn't believe it. He lived in her city or at least close to it. How could she meet him? If she started in his direction was there a chance of meeting him in the thousands of people who were milling around. What would you say if she did? *Hey, I am your soul mate. I bet you have been looking for me.* A man like him would definitely have a date. That would be awkward. Her eyes drifted toward her date.

Gavin smiled at her, unaware that her thoughts focused on another man. He gave her lavish compliments that made her cringe a little. A sincere compliment always worked better than declarations of no other woman was as beautiful. He was a decent enough man. There should be no reason they both couldn't have a good time tonight, but a third date was out, especially since she'd seen her soul mate.

Nina enjoyed the concert and even sang along with the songs without being three sheets to the wind. She even stood up and danced a bit to both her and Gavin's surprise. Since she happened to be feeling very sexy, staying sober would probably save her from acting inappropriately. The evening seemed magical as if anything could happen. She knew her mood wasn't due to Gavin's presence, but he would be the recipient if he drove her home. A good thing she'd met him there.

Nina didn't think of herself as the head-turning type, but she was feeling it tonight. The group did an encore, which left many screaming for more. It was time to go. She hesitated, stepping out in the flow of humanity when *he* walked by with another man. Boy, did she read that wrong. Turning to Gavin, she tucked her hand into his, causing him to smile.

"I like a woman who isn't afraid to assert herself. In many cultures, women are the sexual aggressor."

Okay, she was wrong about Gavin's naiveté and obvious her soul mate preferred men to women. His date was very attractive. Could be they weren't together. The man walked behind him as opposed to beside him. It was so confusing. Did seeing him twice tonight count as two meetings? If so, she was up to six, which only left her with one for her entire lifetime. She had to make that meeting count.

Her date hip-checked her and smiled when he got her attention. He guided her through the milling crowd. His hand smoothed up and down her bare arm, barely touching her skin, but stimulating all the same time. A sideways glance confirmed Gavin did have some after concert plans on his mind. It wouldn't be right to use him when she wanted different arms around her. Somehow, she had a feeling he wouldn't mind, but she prided herself on integrity.

They walked to her car where Gavin made his big move. In the darkness, punctuated by small circles of illumination thrown by the security lights, Gavin managed to trap her against her own sedan by caging her in with his arms. He dipped his head for a thorough kiss, she hadn't anticipated. Her mouth dropped open in surprise, which he mistook for compliance and attempted to surge into it while plastering her against her car.

"Hey look. There's a dude who's going for it. Take a lesson." The masculine comment made her cringe and apparently penetrated Gavin's lust-induced stupor enough for him to stop and back away a step. It was long enough for her to see who spoke. She blinked, twice trying to bring the man into focus in the poorly lit parking lot. It looked like the man she thought was her soul mate's date. He didn't sound gay.

Gavin apologized for his behavior, returning to his initial awkwardness. Nina could hear his words, but her eyes were on the tall man walking across the parking lot beside the man who commented. She recognized his shoulders and curling hair. Unbelievable, she knew it was him, Antonius. Oh my God, it might be their seventh meeting. "Wait," she called.

Antonius glanced back, but kept walking. Gavin, who had turned away and started toward his own vehicle, turned with a happy expression. The wrong man stopped. Gavin came toward her with a bit of a swagger. Great, now he thought he was going to get lucky.

"Wait, I forgot to thank you for the concert. Thanks." She waved, jumped into her car before he got close enough to plaster her against it again. Tomorrow in the intense sunlight, she'd check the paint job to make sure no scratches resulted from Gavin's impulsive actions.

She entered the idling traffic, which gave her plenty of time to think. *It can't be the last time. I refuse to allow it to be the last time. I am smarter than the average bear. There has to be a way to meet my soul mate.* She knew they went to the same schools, even college. Apparently, he lives in a nearby neighborhood, or he wouldn't be at her grocery store. The fortune teller had warned her against forcing a meeting, but desperate women resorted to desperate measures.

WALKING ACROSS THE pavement, Tony fought the urge to look over his shoulder. It was the same woman, the one from the store. She cleaned up good. When she looked up at him, there was a spark of recognition. He'd know if he ever dated such a voluptuous armful. He liked his women curvy, which made settling for rail thin Sheila weird.

He couldn't help himself. He looked back. The jerk who plastered her against the car was walking away. Good. He didn't like to think of them together.

Daniel turned to look also. "It's sad when a bro strikes out."

He felt forced to disagree. "Not necessarily. That's the woman, the one in the grocery store."

Daniel walked backward, taking in the woman getting into her sedan.

"Stop it." He shoved his friend. "I don't want her to notice. Well you, at least."

Daniel laughed. "I have to say she looks your type, much more than Sheila ever was."

"Exactly what I was thinking, but how do I meet her? I tried talking to her in the store. I winked at her at the concert. Now, she's gone." He shook his head. Impromptu meetings didn't do very well for Tony, but planning allowed him to pull out the works.

"What did she do when you winked at her?" Daniel asked, while checking out a trio of tipsy women in short skirts.

"She acted like she recognized me, and when I winked her mouth dropped open in surprise. The man she was with started whispering in her ear. Asshole." Just thinking about the man made him grit his teeth. The fact they came in separate cars meant they weren't serious, which secretly pleased him.

Daniel turned to look at the long line of traffic. He pointed to a dark sedan creeping out the parking lot with the speed of a snail. "That's her car. Catch up with her. She'll probably let you in. It sounds like she's interested."

Tony found himself running after the car pointed out to him. What if she didn't want to talk to him? Tapping on a car window might cause him to be mistaken for a stalker or worse. He reduced his jog to a walk as he came closer to the car. All the cars had to slow to navigate the traffic circle. He needed to reach her before she entered the circle. Dashing in front of a few creeping cars, he earned a few horn blasts and one-fingered salutes. He neared the expensive sedan as the tinted window suddenly moved down, allowing the driver to toss out a cigar. A cigar? He crouched to look into the car only to see a middle-aged man and his wife staring out at him.

"What's your problem? Are you some kind of a voyeur?" the man asked.

He would remind Daniel later he needed to get his eyes checked. "Um, no, I was trying to catch up with my girlfriend."

The man grunted, while his wife looked sympathetic and said, "Drove off without you, you poor thing. Leaving a prime article like you on your own isn't smart."

"You're so right, ma'am," he agreed, before turning to retrace his route at a much slower pace.

Daniel leaned against the car with his arms folded and a somewhat apologetic look. "Wrong car. I saw her turn the other way after you took off running."

"You didn't try to stop me? The man I stopped could have come out of the car swinging." At least he had the car key, preventing Daniel from taking off and stranding him while he'd chased down the wrong car. It would be a suitable ending to a fruitless night.

The full moon made it the perfect romantic setting. Of course, he was missing the necessary component, a woman.

Daniel whistled low and long. "You run fast. Do you seriously think I could catch up with you? With the added incentive of a female, you ran even faster. Waiting by the car seemed like the best thing to do."

Pushing the fob button, Tony unlocked the car. Did he even need the complication of a mystery woman? His life was complicated enough already. He started his prized Mustang with a full-throated purr, using all eight cylinders and dual exhaust to announce its presence. The convertible top folded back, allowing in the moonlight.

Daniel rested his arm on the open windowsill. "I am surprised Sheila didn't complain about this babe magnet mobile."

"She didn't say a word, which I thought was strange. A few of the men at work commented on how their wives would never let them

THE SOUL MATE SEARCH

have such a hot car, but it just didn't seem to matter to her. Maybe she felt she couldn't complain since she was out doing who knows what. Ironically, we lived very separate lives for people living together. She needed me until she didn't." He shifted the car into first and worked his way into a long line of traffic.

Daniel waved to a few women walking to their cars, one waved back. "Why did you two move in together again?"

"Funny you should ask. I was trying to remember myself." He inched the car forward, ignoring all the women who responded to his friend's gestures. A few acted interested, the ones who'd been drinking too much in his opinion. They gave him and his car the once over as if they were a package deal. Not interested, he'd had enough of serving as a hostel and bank for women between relationships.

Daniel looked away from one older woman who waved enthusiastically at him. Instead, he pretended to be in deep conversation. "Did you suggest moving in together?"

"It would be a standard assumption. We were not even a couple technically. We went out on a few dates, which at best were fair. No great passionate love affair, then she starts talking about her roommate leaving. How she couldn't afford her apartment. I suggested she could live with me until she found a new place. We weren't a great couple who couldn't stand to be apart. I was trying to be a nice guy." His leg was starting to ache from riding the clutch. Couldn't hit the open road soon enough.

"So when did you become a couple?" Daniel levered his seat back so he faced the stars.

Tony snorted as he tried to decide what defined a couple. "I would say it was the time she crawled into bed with me, but Sheila must have seen it differently."

"Well, now it's all history. You were always a weird couple. She

35

never hung onto you at parties or glared at women she thought might be scoping you out. Sometimes, I figured she had to be amazing in bed to keep you around."

"Nope, she wasn't. All she had to be was there, which she was mostly. It was convenient to have her watch the house when I was gone and take care of Sebastian too. If Sebastian hadn't died, you'd be stuck with a Great Dane and me both crammed into your small place."

Daniel pretended to shiver in horror. "Most girls like dogs. It's a great way to meet females."

A gap opened enough for him to tap the accelerator. "You know I appreciate you letting me crash with you, but don't you ever think of anything besides sex. You never stay with anyone long enough to get to know them. Don't you want more?"

"If you're asking if I want to be used the way Sheila used you, no thank you." Daniel folded his arms, demonstrating his mood.

"No, not like that. As for Sheila, I guess you can say we used each other. I took advantage of her house and pet sitting service, with an occasional side benefit of sex. She used me for credit rating, rent, and maybe to keep her mother off her back. In the end, her mother was asking me when we would bless them with grandchildren. Don't you want the whole deal where someone loves and adores you? Your partner on life's journey? A regular soul mate? The two of you make a whole?" He liked the way it sounded. Yeah, that was what he was looking for. His satisfaction vanished with his friend's laughter.

"Sounds like we need to stop by the drugstore and get you some PMS medicine."

He delivered a quick slap to Daniel's stomach. "Oops, my hand slipped."

"Don't maim me because the women love me," Daniel teased, while using his arms to block any additional blows to his midsection.

"Hey, I'll help you find your mystery girl."

If anyone could track her down, Daniel could. His official title was IT Technician, but hacker suited him better. He found dozens of girls' numbers who did not freely offer them. Surprisingly, they went out with him, convinced they had given him their numbers. He seemed to like the dim bulbs or they were the only ones who agreed to a date.

"How are you going to do it?" He imagined him going through various databases.

"Do you know her name?"

"No."

"Where she lives?"

"No." He didn't like where this was heading.

"Okay, it looks like we'll be hanging out at the grocery store near my house."

He looked away from the car in front of him to stare in disbelief. "That's your plan?"

"Watch it."

The bumper of a blue sedan loomed in front of him. He hit the brakes in time to avoid hitting the car, but ended up stalling the Mustang. *Damn it*, he hadn't killed the engine since he started driving. He managed to get the car going while wishing he hadn't put the top down to put his stupidity on display. They drove in silence for a while until they managed to peel off to a side road.

They reached a cruising speed of fifty, making conversation difficult. With the wind factor, it resembled yelling on a roller coaster as opposed to actual conversation. Their voices tended to drift behind them. No one was behind him, which was good.

"I can't hang out in a parking lot. Besides having to work, my lawyer called. I'm going to take the house back. We're bringing in the sheriff as Sheila leaves so she only takes her stuff."

"Sheriff, huh? Did you buy anything together?" Daniel held his arms over his head to feel the wind.

His friend could be such a child at times. On the other hand, he must have been born prematurely old. "No, I can't think of a thing. I had everything already and nothing broke. All she ever bought was clothes and shoes."

"You two were the most un-couple I have ever run across. If I were a woman," Daniel flashed a grin, "I'd settled down with you in a heartbeat. You're handsome, a hard worker, thoughtful, and relatively tidy. I am going to assume you aren't too selfish in the sack, either."

"I'm not." He assured his friend, but there had never been any great passion between Sheila and him. No effort on his part to be the best lover she had ever had, either. Why should he if she was just providing rent sex? The way he tolerated the behavior for so long made him sick. Tony realized he'd promoted his career over his love life, and Sheila was the inevitable consequence. The only good thing about Sheila was he'd put no effort in courting her. Some man might feel like he stole her, but there was nothing there to steal.

"Daniel, I am weirded out over you finding me attractive." He joked while his friend made a face in response, one involving gagging. "That's overkill. You might hurt my feelings. I am vulnerable right now."

"Please, I know better. You were probably vulnerable for all the time you were with Sheila. Not so much now. You've decided you wanted something better. If it happens to be the mystery girl, then I love her already." He threw his arms wide as he shouted his love for the unknown woman.

"I accept you consider yourself a pickup artist but hold off declaring your love for her at least until I find out her name."

He flicked on his turn signal to turn into Daniel's neighborhood when Daniel shouted. "Look, it's her!"

A sedan in front of them turned the opposite way. It might be her. Did he really want their first meeting to be with a police escort? He hesitated a moment, watching the car turn left. "What's in that direction?"

Daniel scratched his neck as the wind ruffled his hair. Tony was about to repeat the question when he answered. "Not a whole lot, a few farms, an access road to the bottling factory. If you go far enough, a gated community a couple miles down the road, Heaven's Gate or something.

He completed his turn into Daniel's adult community for people without children, but plenty of disposable income. There were several lights on in the various condominiums and laughter drifting over from the pool area. The complex boasted several other amenities including a well-equipped gym and spa. He could see why it appealed to Daniel. In high school, he was the quintessential nerd most girls overlooked. In college, he put on some weight and bulked out.

"That's it!"

"What?" Daniel asked, although his attention stayed more on the pool activity. Two women in bikinis ran around the pool perimeter pretending to shriek, laughing between screeches.

"I saw the mystery woman at college. I'm sure of it. She was trying to carry this enormous box, and I carried it for her." Because she somehow seemed to be an integral part of who he was—which didn't make sense—it helped to be able to place her.

"Did she thank you? Did you catch her name?" Daniel focused on the women at the pool looking like they were trying to make as much noise as possible.

Tony considered briefly leaving the top down and canvassing the gated community. He discarded the plan almost immediately. They probably had a guard who would call the police if he saw his car one too many times. Nope, he might as well leave Daniel to his hacking magic. Pressing the roof button, he waited for the top to close before locking it in place. "To answer your question, I left the box at her room, Morris Hall 214 J."

"You never went back? Never got your gratitude kiss?" Daniel stopped ogling the women long enough to stare at him in disbelief.

He stepped out of the car, locked it, and *did not* share any enthusiasm for scrutinizing what he judged to be jailbait. "C'mon, I would like to go to bed. You can come back out later and look at girls young enough to be your daughter."

Offended, Daniel pushed in front of him to open the door. Tony was surprised his friend had followed him. "No more poolside voyeurism for you."

"No." Daniel collapsed into a chair and picked up the remote. He went through a series of channels before settling on a western-theme movie. "I can't enjoy it when you make me feel like a dirty old man."

Knowing he'd upset him, he sat down on the couch, wondering how to make it right. His eyes traveled over the black leather furniture and the abstract paintings, all leaning toward the chaotic side. A couple of silk plants softened the effect. An enormous widescreen television dominated one wall. The overall effect was a classic bachelor pad. Tony wouldn't be surprised if there weren't instructions online detailing how to create one. Daniel's kitchen table was more like a bar table with its high top and equally high chairs. Eating was not a priority here or at least not at the table.

"Danny," he started, feeling the look of death directed his way. "I know you weren't tight with the girls in high school, but you were a nice guy, a fun guy. Then you started putting on some muscle and became this alpha guy Daniel, a regular love and leave 'em type. I doubt you've dating anyone more than four times."

"Three," his friend corrected. "I only go out with them three times at the most, or they suddenly think we have a relationship. Can't have that."

THE SOUL MATE SEARCH

"Why? You know we are both turning forty, and then it will be fifty. Will you still be ogling females young enough to be your daughter or trying to pick up drunken women for mediocre sex, and then you refuse to call them later? Do you feel like it's payback for some girl who ignored you in high school or college?" The words kept tumbling out of his mouth, things he'd thought, but never said.

"Antonius, if this is your idea of cheering me up, you majorly suck." He pushed to his feet and turned off the television. "I'm going to bed. I'm not sure I can take much more of your cheer."

"Wait," he called, trying to stop him. A memory of a more feminine voice calling out "*Wait*" crystallized in his mind.

Daniel turned expectantly.

He remembered the tone of her voice calling. Did anxiety or desperation flavor the word? Was she calling him or the man who'd plastered her against the car? A person would think since she drove away without her date that she was calling him or he only wanted it to be true.

Daniel cocked his head and looked at him curiously.

"Oh, I was trying to make a point. Danny was a dude many women would be proud to call sweetheart. Too bad, no one ever meets him."

Daniel put his hands together in a slow applause. "Good effort. I went from fourteen to twenty-two being Danny, and it got me one and a half dates. One woman actually left halfway through the date after boxing her food after it arrived. The full other one wasn't much better. Somehow I convinced her to go back to her ex."

It would do no good to try to reason with him and remind him the girl who left early had actually been sick. He wanted the old Danny back for selfish reasons. To have a friend who did more than ogle women or try to figure how fast he could slip their panties off. At least Daniel could help him track down his mystery woman.

Chapter Four

HER KNUCKLES SHOWED white against the black leather-wrapped steering wheel. She tried to relax her fingers. Inhaling deeply, she mentally searched for her happy place. An image of a beautiful beach with a shimmering sea filled her mind as she idled in traffic. Breathing slowly she relaxed. She strolled her deserted island, and there he was in a pair of loose linen pants, rolled up to his knees. His hipbones barely held the pants up. His open shirt revealed an intriguing trail of hair running beneath the barely-staying up-pants. A sharp tug would surely de-pants him. She knew he was commando. It was her happy place, wasn't it?

A car horn startled her. She'd allowed a gap to develop between her and the next car. Pressing the gas pedal, she closed the space. She needed to keep her mind on traffic until she got home. Instead, her mind considered Gavin's behavior.

"Well, it was a surprise. I didn't think he had it in him." She often talked to herself in the car. It helped her to work out issues. She figured most people assumed she was on the phone and the others didn't care.

Her first desire was to call Ellie, but this was her date night with Justin. Just because her own love life sucked, was no reason to impair her friend's romance even if the guy was a jerk. Concert traffic finally gave away to a lonely drive home. Earlier in the evening, for a moment, she'd considered bringing Gavin home for a little mattress frolic. After he practically forced her in a parking lot, she needed to rethink his potential. It appeared he had none. Better to find out now.

Emails from other men sat in her online dating mailbox. In some ways, she was like catnip to them, or would be if they were cats. Her seeming lack of interest inspired them to write letters copied from romance novels. She should consider one of them. She wasn't getting what she wanted, and they couldn't be any worse than Gavin.

Fate could be a cruel bitch, tempting her and yanking the man away. She slowed for the stop sign. Something told her to glance in her mirror, and she saw him driving a Mustang convertible with his friend. He stared at her sedan, while he idled at the turn-in for the adults only complex. *Party City*, she heard others call it. Others named it *Orgy Capital*. Knowing where he lived was a disappointment. She could have sworn their eyes met in her mirror, which was silly. It was too dark. No way, he could see her, but she still felt his eyes on her. She turned left, hoping he'd follow her. He didn't. It would be foolish if he did. Was he under the impression she was his soul mate? She doubted it.

Everything about her home mocked her as she pulled into her garage. It was too big for one person. She forgot to leave a light on, but a light flickered to life as she entered the foyer. There were too many unused rooms for a killer to lie in wait. Why a killer would hide in her house made no sense. No one wanted to kill her. She hadn't stolen anyone's man, corrupted any minors, or significantly ruined anyone's business. Unless, their recent suit sale was taken into account. At best, a few menswear store managers may have used her name in vain, but not exactly a killing matter.

She had thoroughly spooked herself, which made her go through the ritual of checking every room. "God, I need a dog." The words bounced off the ceramic Italian tile kitchen floor. She surveyed the room for possible felons. None unless they were crouched into the cabinets. A shiver went up her spine. Why did she have to add that imagery to her repertoire? On to the spare bedroom and bath, the living room, her office, and the room she intended to be her exercise room but never used. No visible killers but they would probably hide, wouldn't they?

"Stop that," she muttered to herself.

Returning to the kitchen, she poured herself a small snifter of brandy. She held it aloft, toasting herself. "This is for surviving an evening with Gavin." Truthfully, it hadn't been bad until he started pawing her. She could probably expect abject apologies tomorrow. Her phone chirped. Make that tonight. She ignored it.

Still holding her glass aloft, she announced to the silence, "To the soul mate search, may I emerge triumphantly."

The brandy went down sweet and thick, warming her insides and filling her with hope. It would happen. She knew it would, but not tonight. She shut off the lights as she walked to her bedroom. Turning on her bedside light first, she turned off the overhead. Kicking off her heels, she knew she should pick them up and place them in her closet. She didn't feel like it. Her dress joined her shoes on the floor. Her strapless bra and panties followed.

Even though she might be feeling rebellious, she padded to the bathroom to wash off her makeup. No good would come from wearing makeup to bed. Oh, she was a wild one all right. Her toothbrush cleared away the residual flavor of brandy. Time for bed and *Bob*. She opened her bedside drawer, removing a purple vibrator and a bottle of lube. Bob had the distinction of variable speeds, pulsing action, rotating head, and lasted as long as eight hours until his batteries began to falter. She placed Bob's base between her closed thighs. Squeezing a dollop of lube in her hand, she raised it to her nose, strawberry. Her tongue touched the slippery consistency of the liquid and tasted the artificial strawberry tang. Not real berries, but something like them with a boatload of chemicals added.

According to the bottle, the lube would work for all sorts of sexual play. Rubbing her hands together, she heated the lube between her hands. She stroked it on the purple penis shaped vibrator, pretending she stroked her soul mate as opposed to her rubber boyfriend. Bob was always ready unless she forgot to replace his batteries. He didn't insist on a favorable play-by-play review of his performance, either.

The last forty-eight hours consisted of her thinking about her soul mate. As her soul mate, she assumed they would be a perfect match in bed. Her restrained hairstyles and business suits might make people think she was an ice queen in the bedroom. They'd be wrong.

Closing her eyes, she imagined Antonius above her. Antonius sounded so ancient. She would call him Anton or Tony. He'd put his glasses on the side table, the better for her to see into his gorgeous brown eyes. His biceps bulged as he held himself over her, waiting to plunge into her.

"Now," she whispered to her imaginary lover, vigorously thrusting Bob in and out until she came in a burst.

Falling back against her feather pillows, she allowed Bob to roll across the mattress. Tomorrow morning, she'd clean Bob. Tonight, she needed sleep and maybe to dream of the man she was determined to find. Turning out the light, her eyes closed, and she immediately drifted into a dream.

A fog surrounded and swirled around her, making it difficult to see. She held out her hands and encountered glass. She was inside the crystal ball. "Help me, Helen." A large eye blinked at her through the glass. Her mouth moved, but no sound came through. Perhaps she could read her lips. "Fate cannot be altered." What did that mean?

Did fate place her in a crystal ball? She doubted it. A flash of someone moving through the fog caught in her peripheral vision. It was him. How lucky could she get? Nina called out to him, "Tony, Tony, over here!"

He stopped when he heard this name. Up close, he was even more magnificent than she thought. His eyes were larger without his glasses, his nose a trifle longer, but it looked good on him. "Who are you? How did you know my name?"

She was hurt he didn't recognize her even in the dream world. "I'm your soul mate."

His head turned, and he blinked as if trying to focus. "I can't see you. You can't be my soul mate."

"I am. I know I am." Panic threatened to overwhelm her. He needed his glasses to realize he'd found his soul mate. She patted down his clothes, searching for them.

"What are you doing?" A touch of bewilderment caused his eyes to roll wildly in his head.

This wasn't going well. It certainly wasn't the dream she planned on having. "I am searching for your glasses so you can see I'm your beloved."

He covered her searching hand with his. "Don't bother looking. I'm blind."

Unexpected! She never thought her soul mate to be less than perfect. Too many movies for her. "How will you recognize your soul mate then?" His lips turned up into a beautiful smile. "My heart will know her. I will recognize her by her love."

By her love? How sweet was that? She plucked out one of her eyes, removed his blind orb, and replaced it with her good eye. It was surprisingly easy. Her hand hovered at her last remaining eye ready to pluck it out too.

"No, wait, I can see you. My own true love. My Soul Mate. We can

share your eyes." He held his arms wide, and she walked into his embrace.

All was well, despite doing optical surgery without any anesthesia. Call it a learning curve.

She slept through the night, feeling arms embracing her and his head behind hers, resting on the pillow. She'd swear she heard the gentle sounds of breathing, not her own. Dawn came too early, reminding her she went to bed later than usual.

Her first thought was it was Sunday. She couldn't go to the fortune teller's place. Helen could have weekend hours. After all, one never knew when a person might want an emergency reading. It would be easy to do if she lived on the premises. Perhaps she could talk Ellie into going with her to prove she wasn't crazy. That's what she'd do. The clock numerals glowed a red 7:12. Too early, to do anything or maybe to convince anyone to do anything.

Instead, she retrieved the Sunday paper delivered by a young man who lived in the community. His parents probably thought it would build character. No matter, she was just glad to have her paper. The coffee aroma drifted from the kitchen, making her very thankful for an unknown salesperson who left her a gift of sublime coffee. She should give the man a hearing even if she found the suit line name odd. There had been worse, including the *Gladiator* and the *Capone*. Neither one did well. Men didn't enjoy anything historical about their clothing unless it was a war re-enactment.

She knocked out three miles on the treadmill with an unusual amount of energy. Despite her odd dream, she felt hopeful. He was close, possibly even in the sleazy adult complex, but she refused to consider it. The eerie vision referred to him not being able to see something clearly because obviously he had two working eyes even if he needed glasses.

After a shower and a breakfast of peanut butter toast, she figured she waited long enough even if the boyfriend stayed over. Of course, the two of them would want to have a leisurely breakfast and spend the rest of the day together. Ellie confided on a good day, Justin was gone before eight am to get the best tee time. Lucky for her, it wasn't raining.

A breathless Ellie answered the phone. "Hello."

"Hello, Sunshine. Ready for a wild adventure to the other side?"

"Oh, it's you."

The greeting sounded like she was the last person her friend wanted to hear from. "I love you too."

Ellie sighed. "Never mind. I thought you were Justin, but you aren't. We fought. He called me a controlling bitch and stomped out of the house."

"Was this before or after you served him a delicious gourmet meal you spent all day preparing?" She'd place money it was after. The man played Ellie like a well-tuned fiddle. For the most part, she kept her opinions to herself after Ellie accused her of jealousy. She'd rather be alone than put up with the type of nonsense the narcissistic man dealt out.

"After," Ellie said, punctuating her answer with a few sniffles.

"Sweetie, you need something to get your mind off the man. How about a trip to the fortune teller, followed by a champagne brunch?"

Nina knew Ellie had been needling the boyfriend to take her to a champagne brunch for a while. Of course, he never did.

The delighted giggles made her smile. It didn't take too much to excite her friend. A man who cared might try to make her happy, but she never attracted those kinds of men. They must be an endangered species.

"What should I wear?" Ellie gushed, suddenly giddy like a child.

A few who believed white gloves and hats were mandatory for

champagne brunch, but the masses with credit cards invaded with their Bermuda shorts, flip-flops, and loud Hawaiian shirts.

"A summer dress with a pair of dressy sandals will serve. Maybe a sweater. I hear the air conditioning can sometimes be a bit much. I'll swing by in forty minutes, okay?"

"Yes, yes," Ellie vigorously agreed, almost as if she were fist pumping her answer.

That was easy. Nina thought it might be hard to convince her friend of the need to see Helen, but mention a champagne brunch and suddenly everything was golden.

She pulled out a pansy decorated halter dress with a full skirt. It reminded her of something 1940s starlets might wear. Not suitable for work, but definitely could work for a champagne brunch, along with a lace jacket. She slipped on a pair of heeled sandals. A stroke of mascara and a smear of lip gloss should do the job. Her skin needed time off for the weekend too. She brushed her long hair in preparation of twisting it up on her head, but decided to leave it down, something she almost never did. A silk flower comb was the only thing holding the thick waterfall of hair back. The full-length mirror reflected back a beautiful, confident woman.

Ellie waited on the steps of her condominium, clutching a purse matching her classic pumps. She looked more heading to church than getting tipsy with the upper crust set. Nina stopped the car and unlocked the passenger side door.

Her friend jumped in the front, talking at the same time. "You think I didn't hear what you said about the fortune teller. Well, I did. I figure I've fixed Justin gourmet dinners, provided him with excellent sex for the last few months, and yet, no champagne brunch. It was something I've always wanted.

Nina laughed as she eased the big car out of the neighborhood. "You are so easy."

Ellie leaned back into the upholstery closing her eyes, sighing heavily. "You know, apparently I am free now. I could use a date like you, someone who knows how to show a girl a good time."

"So that's the way it is. Promise me you won't go running back the first time he crooks his finger." As great as Ellie was, she had the dreadful habit of taking back loser men. Often she wondered if a neon sign was above her front door, reading *Losers Apply Within*.

Ellie agreed to forgo Justin's overtures, as they turned onto the street where the shop was. She slowed the car, replaying the route. There was the yoga studio next to the remnants place. Wait, where was it? No one was on the street, not a car, not a person. Sunday wasn't a busy day on the commercial avenue. She eased into two empty spots. Parallel parking was never her strong point.

"Where's the shop you talked about? Some type of junk shop you said." Ellie twisted in her seat, trying to locate it.

It wasn't there. Something wasn't right. "I think I'll walk the block. Could be I was driving too fast."

Ellie crawled out of the car to join the search. "All dressed up in this neighborhood, they'll think we're high-class hookers." The remark made her giggle.

Nina was unwilling to admit she couldn't find the shop. They both walked to the closed spice shop in their high heel sandals. The small shops huddled together like gossiping sisters. It was on this side, she knew it. Heat rose from the pavement, which wasn't too unusual for summer in the city, warming her feet through her thin sandals. Walking on hot concrete wasn't the sandals' original purpose. Three times, she passed where the shop should be. Nothing.

A police cruiser came deliberately up the street and eased in front of her car. A window came down and a smiling officer leaned out. "You ladies lost?"

The other officer had the courtesy to get out of the car and walk around it to meet them. The tall officer knew he looked fit and sexy in his uniform and wasn't above using it to his advantage. "Can I help you, ladies?"

Nina had mentally dubbed Officer Yummy, and Ellie looked like she wanted to grab him, throw him in the back of the car, and make a run for it.

"Well, uh, Officer." She edged closer, not wanting to share her confusion with Ellie. "I was looking for a fortune telling shop. A woman there reads Tarot cards and sometimes crystal balls. Do you know where it is?" She pointed over her shoulder. "It was there."

His partner, who listened intently, shook his head dismissively. "You are the third person this month looking for that shop. Every person swears it was there and she'd gone inside. Apparently, the woman gives you valuable information, but no one was willing to tell me what she said. How about you?"

Nina wasn't ready to volunteer information, either, especially if the man thought she was crazy. Ellie wasn't so hesitant.

Stepping up to the tall officer, Ellie looked up and smiled in a dreamy fashion. "She told Nina about her soul mate. Said she already met him three times, and she only had four times left. She has to see what he looked like in the crystal ball to know what she was looking for. Anyhow Nina messed up when she saw him at the grocery because…"

Nina placed a warning hand on her friend's arm. "Brunch," she reminded.

Ellie turned to her. "I know about brunch, but this is serious stuff if you lose all your chances to find your soul mate." She turned back to the officer and smiled again. "We just need to know if Nina gets at least one more chance."

Officer Yummy tried to maintain a serious demeanor while his partner grinned. "I personally guarantee that you," he pointed to

Nina, "will get dozens of chances dressed as you are. One of them will be your soul mate. You said you know what he looks like?"

"I do. I went to school and college with him. I interviewed him for a job. He winked at me last night while I was with my date, which didn't work out well. Um, sorry I am rambling." Her cheeks flushed.

The younger officer touched his hat, "You ladies have a nice lunch."

Ellie waved and agreed with a touch too much enthusiasm. "We will, Officer."

In the car, with the air conditioning on, Nina felt safe enough to hiss. "God! Ellie, was there anything you didn't tell them?"

"The man was so tall, official, and handsome. I felt overwhelmed to confess everything, including my fantasies about men in uniform."

Nina shifted the car into gear. The lack of shop troubled her. If there was no Helen, did it follow she had no soul mate. The man existed. She saw him several times. Could she be dreaming? She made sure the police had left the area before making a U-turn.

Should she settle for the Gavins of the world? No, she wanted her soul mate. In the end, shouldn't she toast to a triumphant ending to her search? Didn't the officer tell her she could find a soul mate the way she was dressed? Well, she would make it happen.

Chapter Five

TONY THREW AN arm over his eyes to block the light filtering through the blinds. The air mattress stuck to his skin as he rolled away from the light. The sheet had slipped off sometime during the night, probably when he was having strange, vivid dreams about being blind. *Peculiar.* He couldn't blame it on alcohol, either. He was stone cold sober when he went to bed, especially when he realized he'd insulted one of his oldest friends. Greeting Danny, make that Daniel would be difficult this morning. His intention wasn't to offend, but to resurrect the person who enjoyed science fiction books, restoring vintage cars, and making horrible puns. The lothario, who only wanted to screw girls, then dump them, made him uneasy. Sometimes he wondered if he'd get a rep for being similar, just by staying with him. Tomorrow, he'd be back in his own house. The wheels of justice moved very slowly in his case. He'd spent almost a month sticking to an air mattress while Sheila made free use of his house.

Luckily, he had a copy of his household inventory for insurance purposes tucked into his car trunk. The insurance company had a copy too. He faxed one to his lawyer and the sheriff. The way he saw it, he'd been more than generous. It didn't seem unreasonable to want to keep his stuff. He wouldn't bother to litigate, however, if she took off with some small items just to keep her gone. In a way, he deserved it. On some level, he'd known she was a manipulator. Even though he was being used, he liked the idea of having someone waiting for him when he returned home. That in itself was a joke. She usually wasn't there. Sebastian, his dog, saw her more than he had. He wondered what she told the men she brought to his house. His hands fisted at the thought. Definitely had to sell the house, not because the woman broke his heart or even used him, which she did. The space felt violated. The place he lovingly restored was the site of illicit trysts. For all he knew the men friends she brought to his house could be married.

The bedroom door swung open, revealing Daniel in a pair of khakis, polo shirt, and slip-on boat shoes. The stubble was gone, and his combed back hair reminiscent of a preppy as opposed to a bad boy. This was a change. Better yet, he was smiling. During the night, Tony had mysteriously managed to get out of his bad graces.

Daniel stepped into the room and yanked the thin cover off Tony. "Rise and shine, buddy boy. We got places to go."

Pushing up to his forearms, he considered his friend's outfit. It didn't make sense. "This is Sunday, isn't it? Did I sleep through an entire day?" The thought of it being Monday had him rolling onto the floor in a hurry. He had several sales calls to make, but he needed to snag his new contact with Bradley first. If he went early, he might snag the buyer. That's the ticket.

Standing, he walked to the closet attired only in his boxer briefs while Daniel smirked at him. "It is Sunday. You have not slept through the day. I am doing you an enormous favor by cleaning up my image." He gestured to his attire with his graceful swish of his hand.

Tony stopped browsing through his many suits to stare. Holding an open hand to his chest, he said, "You cleaned up for me? I'm honored. What did I do to deserve this?"

"Good you should ask." Daniel interlocked his hands behind his back and began to pace around the golf clubs and suitcase.

Seeing the case, Tony had to grimace. Good thing he hadn't unpacked his car, or he'd be here with nothing. The company gave him plenty of suits to wear, but every now and then, he liked something more casual. "I did ask."

Daniel shot him an amused look before continuing. "I thought about what you said last night. Thought about it a lot. I realized I never gave anyone a chance to know Danny. I tossed a woman out often before she knew my last name. I even had to move a few times so my dates wouldn't find me. A few were reasonably sober. Thinking back on it, it was fun in the short term, but it is starting to wear thin. I can understand what you want. Maybe I might want something similar. So I got up this morning, took what I knew, a woman with an expensive car who lives in a gated neighborhood, and I came up with something."

"What?" It seemed unbelievable a man could come up with anything with the tiny bit of information.

"Ah ha, I hear the doubt in your question," Daniel teased. He put both hands on his hips and gave him the once over. "While some women might admire your manly form, you will have to get dressed up for champagne brunch at the Garden Pavilion."

"Champagne what? Garden what?" None of this made sense. How would it help me find her? Finding her wouldn't make her like him. He'd be lucky if she'd talk to him. People assume salespeople were so smooth. Some were. When it came to selling suits, he was. Most women he met were by accident. Loosely translated he wasn't trying to land them, but they seem to appear by his side. There hadn't been dozens, far from it. Six real relationships if he considered Sheila as one.

Daniel gestured to his outfit. "This is the look you want for our brunch. A new restaurant offering champagne brunch on Sunday has opened up close to the gated community. Smart business move since most of the patrons come from the neighborhood."

"You found this out how?" True, his friend could unearth info with the best of them, but this was a tad esoteric.

"I called to make reservations, and I mentioned my grandmother who lived the community always enjoyed brunch at this one restaurant, but I couldn't remember the name of it. The reservationist at the Garden Pavilion assured me it was a favorite with the denizens of the neighborhood. It has to be because no one else is close enough, and the buffet is forty dollars a person. You're paying since this is for you."

That last bit explained the smirk. Tony rubbed his hands over his face, trying to wake up. "I'm not sure about this." He picked out a pair of linen pants and a thin long sleeved striped shirt. For the casual look, he'd roll up the sleeves. "I am having lunch with a bunch of blue-haired ladies, and this helps me how?"

"First my friend, you are having lunch with me. We will be at a location close to where your mystery woman was. We will enjoy a delicious repast, and if the dating gods are with us, we may spot her. If not her, there are probably several available high-class women to pick from. We'll probably be the only two men there. It will be like shooting fish in a barrel." Daniel lifted his eyebrows and stuck his tongue out in a juvenile leer.

Tony headed for the bathroom with his clothes in hand. "I understand your motivation now. You do deserve some recompense for putting up with me. Brunch it is."

The shower water beat down on him as he shampooed his hair. First, he'd shave, style his hair, and then splash on the expensive cologne. His mood lifted as he considered the possibility of running into her. She needed a name besides *Her*. She might not like him, a real possibility. He was sure they had met before, besides seeing her at the concert, grocery, and college.

Toweling his hair dry, he remembered a job interview, which didn't happen. The woman was so apologetic she practically stared at the floor. He ended up feeling sorry for her, especially when the other candidate left in a door-slamming huff. He remembered shaking her hand, and for a moment, she looked up showing her beautiful eyes. He remembered feeling a charge and forgetting his disappointment.

That was about the time he changed his name back to the old family name, *Dunn*. His choice came from the desire to distance himself from his father's scandal. His father embezzled from his company and took off with his young secretary. Besides, *Dante*, his mother's maiden name, had a flair, which mattered in the fashion world.

Brushing his teeth, he wiggled his eyebrows in the mirror trying to decide if they were too bushy. Was he as bad as a female? Daniel looked good, not like his usual pseudo bad boy self. If the two of them showed up cleaned, pressed, and coiffed, at a champagne brunch no less, people would assume they were gay.

Daniel would be horrified. He'd keep this tidbit to himself until after the brunch because she could be there. If he had a lucky charm, he'd wish on it. Fate was trying to bring them together. After all, they kept running into one another. Fate, luck, whatever, he hoped was on his side.

Daniel waited in the living room watching an infomercial where three busty women in tiny dresses extolled the virtues of a male potency supplement. Daniel snorted his disbelief at the claims and powered off the television. He turned to eye Tony and gave a wolf whistle. "I don't know bro. I realize we are on a mission for you, but the women will look right through me."

Tony laughed and gave his friend the classic one-arm bro hug. "You flatter me. If you'd stop putting yourself down for a change, you might be surprised what you have to offer. You are good looking, intelligent, at times witty, and didn't you take those ballroom dance lessons?"

His face brightened under the compliments. "I did, although I haven't had a chance to use them as of yet." He took a couple sweeping turns around the living room, his arms cradling his invisible partner.

"Today is your lucky day. I believe you will find your missing dancing partner." Tony didn't actually, but it was nice seeing a spark of the old Danny. Besides, it wasn't too hard to believe.

They kept the top up on the convertible to keep their hair from being windblown. Women might think men's hair was simple, but often it took work. A grinning teenage valet ran out to park their car. Tony eyed the Mustang with some reservations. "Can you drive a stick?"

"Sure thing, sir," he answered.

Tony wasn't convinced until he watched the car move smoothly away. Ok, the kid could drive a stick. He turned to follow Daniel up the stairs just about the time a sedan slid up to the valet station.

NINA WATCHED THE departing man climb the stairs. She recognized his rear view. It sizzled in her memory. "It's him." She nudged Ellie and pointed.

Ellie glanced, but patted her friend's arm. "We talked about this on the way over here. You want to have a soul mate. Who doesn't? To facilitate this soul mate concept, you've invented an imaginary man. Unfortunately, you are seeing him everywhere."

Her best friend thought she was losing it. When she couldn't find the fortuneteller's shop that was bad, but still, it didn't mean she was crazy. The valet walked toward her, opening her door. She exited, giving him her name and keys.

Could Ellie be right? She didn't want her to be right. Today should be about Ellie, as opposed to men who may or may not exist. Didn't the über jerk Justin just dump her? As a friend, she needed to be supportive.

The two of them walked up the steps, where two uniformed employees opened the door. A large tiered fountain encompassed the center of the foyer, forcing patrons to walk single file around it to get to the maître d station.

"Ladies," the man greeted them with practiced warmth. "Do we have reservations?"

"Yes, we do. Look under Bradley." Nina wondered if the smile would disappear if they made the mistake of showing up without reservations.

He consulted his tablet. "Very good. The Garden Pavilion is composed of several rooms. You are in the Magnolia Room. The central brunch is in the Hyacinth Room. Waiters will come to your table to refill champagne and to make omelets to order. This is a leisurely affair so please take your time."

Ellie pranced behind the man escorting them to their table, happier than Nina had ever seen her before. Brunch turned out to be a good decision. She tried to look into the rooms they passed for her imaginary man. If she could just find him and point at him, at least it would prove she wasn't crazy. The maître d kept a spritely pace, making it hard to get more of a glance. All she really saw were women, old women, young women, mothers with teenage daughters. *Wait.* She thought she saw a man, a familiar man. Their eyes met for a startled moment. Not her soul mate, but someone she'd seen before. Didn't she see him with her future soul mate at the concert?

Her moment of uncertainty brought her to a stop, causing both Ellie and the maître d to turn and stare at her. You'd think she'd done something horrendous. They eventually arrived at a small table sheltered by an oversized palm. If couples actually showed up at the restaurant, this is the table they'd give lovers to give them some privacy. Ellie slid into her chair with an excited expression. Her happiness radiated from her, making Nina wonder why Justin Jerk couldn't do this one thing for her friend. Oh yeah, he was a selfish jerk. That explained it. The maître d shook out the napkins, placing them in both women's laps. He winked at Nina, explaining in a low voice that he chose a private table for the two of them.

A private table for the two of them was odd. "Ellie, I think he thought we were a couple."

Her friend's eyes twinkled. "I have to say you are my best date so far. I will overlook the fortune telling thing because I got to stand close to so much uniformed eye candy."

They both were still laughing when a handsome waiter showed up with a magnum of champagne. "Champagne, ladies?" At their nod, he filled their glasses and placed the magnum on their table. "The buffet is in the Hyacinth Room." He gestured in the direction they came from.

"Thank you." She nodded to the waiter who gave a small bow before leaving, impressing Ellie even more.

"Even the waiters are delicious. No wonder Justin never brought me here."

Nina picked up her glass. "Here's to us." They tapped glasses together before sipping. "As for Justin, he never had any intention of taking you anywhere."

Ellie sighed. "You're right. Was he ashamed of me? Am I that unattractive?" She finished the flute in two hasty gulps and poured herself another glass.

Her first instinct was to slow her friend's alcohol consumption, but Ellie probably wouldn't appreciate her efforts. Not a big issue since she was driving anyway. The next best thing was food into her body. "Let's go check out the buffet."

They worked their way through a series of rooms to reach the buffet room with tables full of chafing dishes, fresh flowers, and ice sculptures. Several employees outfitted in chef smocks with tall chef hats stood behind the tables ready to assist. Ellie glanced up at her and mouthed the word, "Paradise."

The place was definitely more about frills and eye appeal than what Nina expected. The business side of her calculated the cost the enormous bouquets of fresh flowers and ice carved swans scattered among the buffet tables. The cost of presentation must pay off in attracting women in droves to the expensive restaurant. An ingenious plan that didn't translate to men's suits.

At the end of the fruit bar, stood her soul mate's friend He turned to leave, catching her eye, but his gaze traveled to Ellie, who absolute- ly transfixed the man. The sight of her friend stopped him in his tracks. Men seemed to love petite women. Leaning closer to Ellie, she whispered, "You have an admirer over by the swan ice sculpture."

Ellie smiled in the man's direction, causing him to flush and duck out of the room. "I did something wrong. He was probably staring at you."

"No, trust me. When he saw you, his whole face changed. It was as if he'd just discovered a precious jewel." She was putting it on thick, but it never hurt for a woman to feel good about herself. The man did act surprised and pleased to see Ellie.

They carried their laden plates back to their table where Ellie chattered, nibbled, and drank. Nina realized on some level she was being a crummy companion. Her thoughts kept going back to

Antonius, whom she had nicknamed Tony. He had to be real. Otherwise, parts of her life didn't exist. He could be no more than a good-looking man she fixated on. Some women might not even like his type. She did though. Her body moistened at the thought of him. A quick trip to the restroom was in order.

"Excuse me, I'll be right back." Her friend saluted her with the flute as a reply.

On her way, Nina noticed some of the women received roses at their tables, which they cooed over. Apparently, you could have flowers sent to the table. Stopping at the maître d's station, she placed an order for Ellie. It would cheer her up and might even slow down her drinking. She tried to word the note so Ellie would think it was from the man who stared at her and asked the maître d to fill it out so Ellie wouldn't recognize her handwriting.

The maître d happily took her credit card, murmuring about romance being in the air. At this rate, she doubted she could ever come back to the restaurant.

In the luxurious women's lounge, she hid in a stall to wipe away the tattle tell moisture. She didn't want to think about what would happen if she actually met him. She'd probably tear his clothes off.

After brushing her hair and checking her makeup, she was ready to finish her brunch. Eager to get back to the table and see Ellie's expression at the flower arrival, she plowed into a man carrying a plate. The plate slipped from his hand shattering on the terra cotta tiles. Oh, my God, she couldn't believe she'd done such a thing. How had it happened? Up to now, she'd always been so careful, so in control. She stuttered, "S-so sorry," barely willing to look up to see whose brunch she had dashed to the floor.

The face staring back at her wasn't angry, only somewhat be-mused. His lips tipped up in a smile. It was Antonius. A dark-haired woman stood behind him. She took a couple steps nearer as if to assert her claim. Several employees came rushing over to clean up the mess, separating the two of them. This wasn't how she wanted to meet. Only seconds ago, she wiped her thighs down due to thoughts of him making her hot and bothered. Now, she barreled into her dream man as if she were a linebacker.

Nina wanted to say something, but she was unsure what? Instead, she retreated, dashing off to the refuge of her hidden table. Ellie greeted her arrival with enthusiasm.

Gesturing to the flowers, she said, "Look what came while you were gone." She pushed the card at her.

"I am so happy for you." Nina forced her lips into a smile. It was difficult. Somehow, she'd managed, yet again, to ruin again her opportunity to connect with her soul mate. He didn't appear angry over her running into him. He was about to say something before she dashed off, but she was too humiliated.

The waiter dropped another magnum of champagne off at their table, which Ellie immediately pounced on. Her friend's excited chatter registered, but she wasn't paying too much attention.

"He sends me flowers just by spotting me on the other side of the buffet line. I've never heard of such a thing. Justin never did anything like that for me. I wish there were some way I could express my appreciation. I could offer him a blow job." Her tipsy giggle indicated she might have had one, two, or three glasses too much champagne.

Her friend definitely had too much to drink. Nina should think about either getting her out of the place or cutting off her alcohol. Her mind flitted back to the man she'd broadsided. Was it the seventh time she saw him? If it were, then she should make a point of finding the man in the restaurant. Since it would be her last chance.

"Nina, what do you think? You didn't answer me when I asked." Ellie cocked her head, waiting for a response.

Great. She hadn't been listening, only thinking about her problems. What kind of friend was she? "It sounds like a great idea." What if she asked about Justin? Better, qualify her answer, "I mean if it doesn't involve getting back with Justin."

Her friend gave her a weird look, shrugged her shoulders, and emptied her flute. "Not for Justin, I'm not that kinky. Besides, he might like it. Okay, here's goes nothing." Ellie pushed up from the table and made a few unsteady steps.

"Sweetie, let me help you." She stood and put a steadying hand on her friend's shoulder.

Her friend shook off her hand, attracting some interest from other diners. "Please, there are some things I can do on my own."

Chastised, Nina sat back down and watched her friend make a circuitous route to the restroom. She could follow at a distance in case her friend passed out in route. Alcohol tolerance did not come naturally to Ellie with her small size.

Chapter Six

DANIEL RETURNED TO the table with his laden plate. He plopped the plate down, causing a grape to roll across the table. "You won't believe who I saw."

Tony continued to chew. He had no doubt he'd hear a detailed description of the latest woman Daniel planned to seduce or at least dream about seducing.

"The girl from the concert." He picked up his fork. "But even better, she had little Ellie McPherson with her. I'm sure it was her. Dressed up in her Sunday best. I had such a crush on her in school. Strangely, she'd always been nice to me, one of the few girls who were."

Tony watched the animation cross his friend's features. It had been a long time since Daniel reacted to anyone or showed any emotion besides an annoying smugness. Nope, most the time he acted as if he were too nonchalant to care. He was glad for him, but needed to clarify who the other woman was. "Explain about the concert girl. Tell me more."

The twist of his lips clearly announced he'd rather wax about the attributes of petite Ellie. "It looked like her. I could be wrong. I don't know her as well as you."

Daniel chewed on a piece of bacon and almost choked. Tony

leaned across the table to deliver several hearty slaps on his back.

"Stop! Enough, I'm okay." Daniel took a swig from his water glass. "Ellie was talking to your mystery woman. We all probably went to the same school. If I made friendly with Ellie, we could discover who she is."

Instead of answering, Tony took a sip of champagne. Did he want this love life balanced on the outcome of Daniel's sleaze ball romantic tactics? The woman probably would have nothing to do with him. "I'll try to win the woman on my own."

Leaving his barely touched plate, he made his way to the buffet, trying to stroll through every room possible. He certainly received more than his share of attention, being one of the few men in the place. The flirtatious glances made him feel like he was part of the offerings.

No sign of her anywhere. Unfortunately, he caught the eye of several dark-haired women while he tried to determine if they were she from the back. They usually turned, indicating whispered cues from their friends. He flashed them an apologetic smile as he made his way to the buffet. It didn't stop one woman from following. She tried to strike up a conversation.

"Hi, I'm Natalie. You looked like you are looking for someone." She grabbed a chilled plate and sidled up to him in line.

His first thought was to ignore her. Miffed women were some-times harder to handle than disappointed ones. "Oh, I'm Tony. My friend spotted some old school pals, and I was trying to find them."

"Women," the woman asked with an arched eyebrow.

Tony seized on the lifeline. "Yes, a woman I've had a crush on most of my life, but we keep missing connections. Maybe this time, we can work things out."

Instead of cooling the woman's ardor, she moved closer. "How romantic! It's hard to find a romantic man nowadays. I knew immediately when I saw you that you were a romantic. I hoped you were looking for me."

Grabbing tongs, he placed fruit on his plate, crowding it with melon and mango slices. He needed to get away from Natalie, who obviously had him in her crosshairs. "Uh, well, I wasn't." He peeled off the buffet line and headed to his table.

Aware of Natalie only a few steps behind him, he hoped to lose himself in the many dining rooms. Here he was, a grown man trying to escape from an amorous woman in the middle of a champagne brunch. Definitely not how he expected to spend the weekend. He glanced at the alarmed expression on the maître d's face before the impact.

The glass plate flew out of his hand, shattering on the floor. That's what he got from trying to escape Needy Natalie. He looked to his right to see who caused the impact only to meet a face he most recently saw in his dreams. She *was* here. His heart leaped. Daniel was right. Give the boy a gold star.

He stared for a moment, taking in her loose hair and halter dress. Damn, she looked like a million bucks plus change. Her expression didn't express joy at bumping into him, instead resembling mortification as she mumbled her apologies and fled.

He stared at her, feeling Natalie closing in on his left flank. A swarm of employees had appeared, picking up the splattered melon and broken glass. Despite the manager's sudden appearance and urging him to replace his spilled food, he didn't. Eating wasn't his purpose in being there. She was.

The maître d stood looking in the direction she fled. "Who is she?" He didn't expect the man to tell him, but it would make things easier. The man glanced at him. "Do not worry. She is with her lover, and they are very much in love. An attractive couple, rather like you and your companion."

She was with her lover. He was too late. *They were very much in love.* His stomach sank. What could he have done differently? His steps slowed. Where did he go from here? Sure, tomorrow he would have his house back, a start at normalcy. Of course, he had his job, but the woman represented so much more. He slid into his seat without speaking. Luckily, his friend was too busy eating to question him.

Daniel's head went up, and his fork dropped from his nerveless finger. Tony turned to see what had such an effect. A petite blonde dressed in a flower-strewn sheath waved. Daniel stood and moved with the calmness and assuredness of someone bewitched. Tony watched Daniel disappear with the blonde-haired woman who had to be Ellie.

Daniel should be very grateful to him. Ironically, the woman came on to Daniel while his love interest fled. This must be where they hide all the randy women. At least, Natalie had stopped tailing him once the maître d made the comment about the woman who ran away being with her lover. No, she'd dropped back at the comment of Daniel and him making an attractive couple, comparing him to the other couple. The only reason he would do that is if he thought both couples were gay.

He motioned for his check. He knew he wasn't gay, which meant whoever she was with probably wasn't her lover, either. Obviously, Daniel and Ellie were together, which meant she was alone some-where in the restaurant. He had to find her. This might be his only chance, considering how things had gone so far with missed opportu-nities sandwiched in between randy boyfriends and stalker-ish brunch women.

The waiter finally came after what seemed like an hour and took his credit card. Tony berated himself for not bringing cash, which he could have left on the table. He looked around, wondering if he could speed the man up. Speed was not a priority for the restaurant. The women lingered over their meals gossiping, holding the waiters as their eager servants until the check arrived.

He strode through the rooms looking for any sign of his woman, Ellie, or Daniel. Near the bathrooms, he found his mystery woman next to the men's restroom with her head angled as if listening. Peculiar. Was she waiting for a lover? Is he jumping to the wrong conclusion? He drew closer to her and the door. He could hear feminine giggling and a masculine voice, which sounded very familiar. *Daniel.* He couldn't take him anywhere.

She looked up at him, glanced at the door, and blushed. "I'm waiting for a friend."

Placing his hand against his chest, he asked, "Is she about this tall, blonde, and giggling?" He cut his eyes to the door.

Exhaling, she nodded. "She's had too much to drink. Her boyfriend dumped her. She's vulnerable."

It's all he needed to hear. Daniel's favorite kind, a sure bet. "I will retrieve your friend. Would you like that?"

"Yes, very much. I would be eternally grateful. I wanted to go in, but the maître d has his eye on me.

His first attempt to open the door failed due to the weight against it, two bodies to be exact. He hissed the words loud enough for them to penetrate, "Danny, I know you are in there. Open the door now."

The door opened and a mussed blonde-haired woman flew out, grabbing his mystery woman in the process. "Go, go!" she pleaded, hooking her arm with the other woman's and dragging her forward.

He watched the woman threw a frustrated look over her shoulder and expressed breathy gratitude.

"Thank you, Tony."

She knew his name. Why didn't he know hers? Daniel exited the bathroom, tucking in his shirt. How could he do this to him? Tony felt like leaving him there. Once again, he missed connecting. It just never seemed to be an appropriate time.

The maître d came beside the two of them, holding up a menu to shield his lecture from the other guests. "The Garden Pavilion is a high class restaurant. We do not engage in shenanigans that are more appropriate to bars and roadhouses. We do not need your patronage. You are not welcome here in the future." He directed the majority of the argument at Daniel.

The maître d turned to Tony and smiled. "You would be welcome with a different companion."

Of course, he would be. Make that his wallet since he'd just paid over a hundred dollars for brunch. Furious, he retrieved his car from the valet, preferring not to talk to his former friend. Tomorrow couldn't come fast enough.

The atmosphere in the car was thick and silent. No way would he be the first one to say anything. Good chance he'd say something and not be able to repair the damage.

Daniel sighed heavily. "Are you willing to hear my side and not think the worse?"

Unwilling to speak, he gestured with his hand to go on.

His friend cleared his throat once. "Well, seeing Ellie wave at me brought back middle school memories. I never admitted to anyone what a major crush I had on her. That's why I rushed to her. It was obvious she was tipsy and horny."

Tony threw him a dark glance. "You didn't?"

"No, I didn't. I think I deserve some credit for resisting. She pulled me into the men's restroom, swearing she was going to give me a blowjob for sending flowers to her table and making her feel better since her guy dumped her." A goofy expression crossed his face.

"You didn't. You said you didn't." The car tires bit into the gravel shoulder, but he guided it back on the road.

Daniel tugged the shirt out of his pants and flapped it to get some air flowing. "Wow, I'm hot. Ellie, for a little thing, is strong. I wasn't expecting her to pull me into the restroom. Then she had me up against the door and was on her knees, unzipping my pants."

Tony grimaced. "I don't want to hear this." Daniel's fist punched his thigh, causing him to depress the gas pedal, jumping the speed. "Could you explain without the theatrics? I want to live another day."

Holding his hands up at shoulder height, he said, "The old Daniel would have taken what she was offering. Instead, I pulled her off her knees. She was tipsy and told me all sorts of things. Her boyfriend dumped her. She didn't care because he never took her to the champagne brunch, and he was lousy in bed. Then she explained she'd spent the morning with her friend, *Nina*, looking for a vanishing fortune teller."

Daniel crossed his arms, looking triumphant.

Her name was Nina. It fit her dark hair. Her full curves suggested an Italian legacy. It would work out well because half his family was Italian. Still, he was back where he started, maybe worse, if Ellie hated Daniel and complained to Nina, who in turn decided he was just as bad by association. It was hard to know how a woman's mind might work. "Does Ellie hate you? She tore out of there, dragging Nina behind her who is probably four inches taller."

Locking his fingers together behind his head, Daniel considered the question. "After I asked her not to go down on me, she was embarrassed but grateful. I told her I'd had a crush on her since junior high. I told her my full name, something I never do, to show her how I felt. She confessed she'd liked me too, but felt like I never returned her feelings because she wore braces." He laughed. "Imagine that."

Turned out his friend wasn't as big a dirtbag as he thought, but where was the part about Nina? "Um, how does this affect me, again?"

Daniel stalled by pulling his knuckles until he cracked each one. Noticing Tony's aggravation, he grinned. "As I said we talked about a lot, rather she spoke, and I made soothing noises. Nina visited a fortune teller, and then the woman's shop vanished. It didn't make much sense to me. Keep in mind, Ellie was tipsy. Here's the central point. She told me where she was going for the Fourth of July, a bash in Nina's neighborhood, and she invited me. Some street party put on by the gated community with fireworks over the lake and all. Nina will be there. Ellie even gave me Nina's code to enter the gate, 4307."

A chance existed. It glittered like gold. How could he make a positive impression? Despite all his failed attempts, he had a feeling she liked him or was interested. It wasn't as if he was inexperienced or stupid. He knew the signs. When they collided in the restaurant, he saw her dilated pupils. Could it be him? He hoped so.

A week before the Fourth and he had a great deal to accomplish. He turned into Daniel's neighborhood without conscious thought anymore. There was screeching by the pool, but this time it was a nuisance, and not an attractive one.

"Do you think Ellie will still want to talk to me?"

That explained his distraction. The Mustang nosed into the familiar guest parking spot. "Good question. You were nice to her, but she humiliated herself. The good news is there will be a few days in between for it to wear off. She'll consider what a great person you are. The good news is you have a prior connection in middle school, which makes it harder for her to dismiss you."

"Prior connection. Interesting."

A female resident popped out her condominium attired in a bikini and waved at both of them.

They both put up a hand, but failed to call out a greeting.

Daniel stared, his jaw dropping. "Why don't you have a prior connection with Nina?"

He shot one hand through his curls. "I've wondered that myself. The best I can figure is we were in different grades."

Sliding the door key into the lock, Daniel opened the door. "It makes sense. If you had a yearbook we could try to look her up."

Males having yearbooks? Only if mothers ordered them. "Nope, don't have one. Tomorrow, I'll find out what I still really have. Sheila has to turn over all the keys to me. I have a locksmith standing by because I don't trust her. Who knows if she has had keys made for all her guy friends?"

Daniel slapped the counter. "It makes no sense. She's in your house while you had to call in the law and police to get your own stuff. Could anyone move into your house and claim it as theirs?"

Using his index finger, Tony rubbed the throbbing spot between his eyes. A headache always started when he considered the energy and time he spent in a non-relationship with Sheila. "Part of it is because we were in a relationship, an acknowledged one by co-inhabiting. Then she told the police she changed the locks because I was abusive. My lawyer commented it is a clever ploy often used by manipulators. They even took statements from my neighbors like I was on trial." Outside of his attorney and his boss, Daniel was the only other person who knew he was locked out of his own house. It wasn't something he wanted advertised.

"Damn, you never said anything about this? Why did you keep quiet? Here I was pushing women at you. Forgive me." He dropped into a chair, shaking his head as if he were the one investigated. "What did your neighbors say?"

"My neighbors had been my neighbors long before Sheila moved herself in. They know me reasonably well, I guess. Ryan said neither of us were ever home at the same time to have fights, which was mostly true. Old Lady Cunningham, the nosy woman whose trees I helped trim—remember her?"

"You said something about she watched everyone. That you always waved when you came home because you knew she was watching."

"True, true. I think the FBI need to hire her. The woman's nosy ways paid off for me. She kept a journal of everyone who came to my home when I was gone. She had dates and descriptions. Once her grandson showed her how to use a digital camera, she had pictures, too, which she shared with the police and my lawyer. Thought it might come in handy. I owe her big. Because we aren't divorcing, there is no settlement. It will be hard returning, knowing all my neighbors are aware of how Sheila played me for a fool." He slumped down on the couch and toed off his shoes.

Daniel scratched his chest and stared off into the distance. "I'd think if you were an abusive man, you'd have gone through a window to get to her. Why did everything take so long? The house is in your name."

"Exactly, but something about possession being the nine-tenths of the law. I had to get her butt out of my house, which takes legal wrangling and apparently the sheriff. My lawyer told me even if she was only a bad renter it would have taken me about three months to get her out. Soon it will be all a memory. A lesson too." He stretched out on the leather couch, listening to it squeak and chirp under his weight. Of course, Daniel would have black leather furniture, part of his macho façade. It would be good to have back his cloth couch that didn't stick to him.

Daniel broke into a chorus about the sun coming out from an old musical. He remembered his friend now. He only wished he could remember Nina from school. The image of Nina casting a glance over her shoulder and breathing out his name, dominated his imagination. How did she know the name he used now? He took his mother's maiden name ten years ago. Only recently had he started calling himself Tony.

A snuffling snore indicated sleep. Daniel's head rested back against the chair, and his mouth gaped open, allowing a series of snores to escape. The thought of taking a snapshot with his camera phone crossed Tony's mind, but he abandoned it almost as soon as it came. Too much, work while he attempted to unravel the mystery of how Nina knew his name.

As a kid, his mother insisted on calling him Antonius, thinking he'd grow into the name. Instead, kids called him Ant and even Onius. Neither name had radiated confidence the way Tone would have. If he had wished for courage, he would have gone with Tone, but he didn't. When he finished college, he felt Antonius would make him sound older and more experienced. That was the name on his résumé, at least the one Nina saw so many years ago.

Ironically, as he grew older and more experienced, he preferred to feel younger and more playful, even if he was a dyed-in-the-wool workaholic. The name might change aspects about him. Purchasing the Mustang convertible and having Sheila move in, he thought demonstrated a more spontaneous nature.

Sheila's arrival was more like an illegal squatter than a girlfriend's. As for the car, he researched it for a year before buying it. Calling it a spontaneous purchase would be misleading.

When did he become so regimented? Even at a young age, he'd made lists and checked off his chores and homework, proving to himself that he'd gotten something accomplished. His paternal grandmother complained his mother was making a nervous nelly out of him by working him so hard. *Boys*, she was fond of saying, *they should go where they pleased, do what they want.* Her philosophy explained why his father, her son, felt no compunction in embezzling from the company that had employed him for over twenty years or leaving his current wife as he and his young assistant headed for parts unknown.

That was the final nail in the coffin for his inner child, impulsiveness, and anything resembling spontaneity. Among his many goals, the biggest one was not to be a screw up like his father. Even though the scandal occurred over a decade ago, no one had heard one word from the man.

His mother divorced her husband in absentia, anxious to remove any legal ramifications to her family. Grandmother Dunn laid the blame for her son's self-serving behavior at his mother's door. His mother's response was surprisingly salty, causing a break between the two families. Too bad, it hadn't happened sooner. It would have made life a little easier for his kind-hearted mother who had tried endlessly to please her mother-in-law, Amanda. Behind her back, she called her *Demanda*. It was their joke his father never knew.

A giant hairy spider crawled into his field of vision as he contemplated the turns his life took. The decent thing would be to get rid of the fellow due to Daniel's spider phobia. The arachnid inched across the ceiling until he slid down a strand similar to a firefighter dropping down the pole and landed on drowsing Daniel's head. The man jerked. "What! What's happening?"

Tony sat up suddenly, ready for the fireworks. Daniel rubbed a hand across his face snagging the arachnid.

"Spider! God, get it away from me!" Daniel scrambled from the chair, dislodging the spider in the process.

Taking a magazine, Tony herded the spider onto it and released it outside on the balcony. That's what friends did, captured spiders, and never ever talked about it.

Chapter Seven

NINA'S HEAD TURNED back to the dark glass doors of the restaurants. It was hard to see inside, to see him standing there, possibly staring. Yeah, he probably have his mouth open in shock. She came with the woman who was providing sexual services in the men's bathroom. Ugh, not an association she wanted she wanted to acknowledge. Ellie tugged at her to get her moving toward her car the valet brought up. This is what sheep must feel like when escorted by a border collie.

"Nina, hurry, I have to get out of here." Ellie's panic caused her voice to warble wildly catching the valet's attention.

Passing him a five-dollar bill, Nina thought of cautioning him to say nothing. Then again, Ellie was not the first distraught woman to ever leave a restaurant. With the flock of high maintenance women inside, there were plenty of meltdowns, usually over divorce settlements or plastic surgery mistakes, not sex in the men's restroom.

She headed for home, thinking it would be better to take Ellie to her house in case the evil Justin made a return visit. She waited until both car doors closed and she cleared the parking lot. "Ellie, today when I saw you I thought you were dressed for church with your matching shoes and purse in your conservative dress, but you sure didn't act like any church lady. What happened?"

The sobs abounded along with the hiccups. Out of the corner of her eyes, Nina could see her friend backhanding her eyes.

"Tissues are in the glove compartment."

Switching on the air conditioning, she listened to the heart-wrenching sobs, wondering when she'd get the real story. Part of it, she'd put on Justin, another part the champagne, the third part of the flirty handsome stranger. Thinking of handsome men made her thoughts drift back to Tony. Why couldn't they ever exchange more than two words? At this rate, it would be lifetimes before they ever got together. Was it her seventh time? She wasn't sure. She never got to talk to Helen again.

Ellie had a tissue in each hand. Her mascara dripped down her face in lines, making her look like an aging rock star. "It's your fault, you and your stupid advice."

Her fault? Really? Here she is, trying to be extra nice to Ellie due to her breakup, and she is blaming her for her uncharacteristic behavior. "How can it be my fault? Did I say go grab the cute guy and have sex with him in the men's bathroom?"

Ellie's lips took a mulish cast as she answered, "Yes."

Nina's fingers tightened on the steering wheel. Mentally she counted to ten in an attempt to diffuse her anger, but heat still crept up her neck. If it hadn't been for Ellie, she might have had a chance to talk to Tony, even set up a date.

"Really, you're going to pin this on me? After you swilled champagne like a sailor on leave. How is this my fault?"

Ellie turned her tear-blotched face to hers with her bottom lip quivering, making her feel like a puppy kicker. "You agreed." She stopped to wipe the tears streaming down her face. Her voice caught, but she pressed on. "You agreed when I asked if I should blow Danny for the roses."

What? Punching in her code to the gate, she tried to make sense of her friend's explanation. "I know I didn't tell you to do that. Not only would it be stupid, it's also skanky."

Ellie's sobs increased in volume.

"Besides, I bought you the flowers. I made the maître d sign the card so you'd think it was from Danny. At least, you know his name."

This remark triggered full-scale bawling. Luckily, her tinted car windows prevented any of her neighbors from seeing her friend dissolving. In this neighborhood, people tended not to come out of their houses. Instead, they drove into three and sometimes four car garages and closed the door. The neighbors who she seldom met didn't matter, but she wanted to save her friend further embarrassment.

"If you bought the flowers, why did you tell me a blow job was a good idea?" Ellie's eyes cut to her accusingly.

The garage door slid open and allowed her to take the discussion indoors. None of this made any sense. Her only resort to calm Ellie down was a rom-com movie along with the emergency chocolate. At least, the distraction would keep her from obsessing on Antonius. "Oh my God, I think I know what happened."

A muffled "What" came from behind a wad of tissues?

Biting her lip, she hated to admit the truth to her friend. "I wasn't listening. Instead, I was thinking about Tony."

Ellie lowered the tissues enough to give her a bewildered stare.

"My soul mate, Antonius, Tony, my dream lover, the man at the concert, the grocery, the man have been obsessed with this entire week." Did Ellie only listen to her one remark?

"Oh, him." The tone of her voice was dismissive.

"Yes, him. He was there. Apparently the guy you pulled into the restroom is his friend." Could it get any worse? First, she knocked his plate out of his hand, and then there was the glowering woman behind him. Then she runs into him again while her friend was making like a barfly in the restroom of the only upscale restaurant in town.

Holding up one finger, Ellie tried to insert, "About that—"

"Let me finish." Opening the kitchen door, she threw an exasperated look over her shoulder. "I am trying to explain what happened. I was busy thinking about Tony and the fact I slammed into him, which was ironic because I'd been thinking about him. Then there was this woman giving me the death stare. I ducked out of there as quickly as I could. You babbled on about Justin."

Her hand on the door, her friend objected. "I don't babble."

Turning her back to her friend, she rolled her eyes. "Okay, what I am trying to say is I may not be paying attention to what you were saying."

Ellie pushed her from behind. "Are you kidding me? We've been friends since grade school. I think you know I'm not Miss Wild and Crazy. I was liquored up, but the one time I come up with a reckless idea, couldn't you have discouraged me?"

Kicking off her heels, she pulled Ellie into a hug. "I was a bad friend. You should be mad at me. You never have to see Danny again, especially after you did what you did."

Ellie muttered something unintelligible into her shoulder. Loosening her tight embrace allowed her to make sense of her friend's words.

Shaking her head side to side, Ellie said, "I didn't do anything, really. I mean I tried to, but he wouldn't let me. Danny pulled me to my feet and called me by my name." A sob threatened to break free.

Putting two fingers to her chin, she pondered the situation. "A nice guy, wow. You lucked out. Not too many men would pass up a tipsy woman offering a free BJ."

"So true." Ellie sauntered to the green and blue brocade couch and threw herself on it. "I am so fortunate." Sighing deeply, she relaxed against the multiple of throw pillows. "I'm feeling really tired." Nuzzling her face into a pillow, she sighed again.

This told her nothing. Danny and Tony knew each other. Danny's connected with Ellie now. The only person not in the circle was her. "When did the guy introduce himself? When he was wrestling back control of his zipper?"

"Ha, ha." Ellie combined her laugh with a yawn. "We knew each other in school. I even had a crush on Danny in middle school. Danny Logan, president of the computer club."

A vague image of a pimply teenage boy with braces and glasses came to mind. As she recalled, he enjoyed verbal puns that caused Ellie to burst into paroxysms of giggles. Remembering the handsome man at the restaurant made it hard to reconcile him with the middle school boy. "Talk about changing. I'd never have recognized him."

Ellie's snuffle indicated she was dead to the world. Oh well, it would probably be best if she slept it off. Work beckoned. Eventually, her friend would awaken and tell her more about Danny and his good friend. At least, she had the possibility of meeting again.

WORK DIDN'T INTEREST her. Closing the accounting screen, she pushed back away from her computer desk. Numbers used to be her solace. Adding them up emphasized her bottom-line and brought her so much contentment. It proved her worth to a certain extent. Most people would say she had no reason to complain. A stable career with regular promotions, an excellent car, and an enviable home in a gated community, but those were just things.

Helen didn't help any with her cryptic warnings about time running out. Nina moved her chair back to her desk, she clicked on an

Internet search engine. Typing *Soul Mate* into the search box, she watch the results fill the screen, 29,000,000 hits. Many people were looking for soul mates or at least they believed they existed. One definition explained that soul mates used to be one person torn asunder because of the choice of self-love over worshipping the gods. The soul mate included two hearts, two faces, two souls that the gods could split in half, casting them far apart.

In one version, the beleaguered souls were blind, making it diffi-cult to find their other half. In still another version, they forgot who their soul mate was, which obligated them to spend the rest of their lives asking strangers if they were their soul mate.

Dating was just another version of the soul mate search. Often she did feel like she was part of the interview process. Who knew the conservative men she dated were looking for a soul mate? Of course, they probably wanted someone as different from their ex as possible, while remaining female.

Most people, mainly women, believed a soul mate knew your heart, your thoughts. Her eyebrows lifted at the words. It would be handy. A man she kept trying to hunt down would know her thoughts and deliver himself to her front door. He'd even know her gate code. She laughed at the sheer absurdness of the thought. Still the heart wants what it wants.

Everyone, it appeared, had an opinion on a soul mate. A few believed you could have several soul mates, which were people you got on with reasonably well while the hardcore thought there was only one, and he or she might not even live on your continent. Helen belonged to the last party she was sure. The woman pointed out that often a soul mate didn't always appear in your current lifetime, never mind country.

Fate was not the fickle bitch she initially thought. Her soul mate was nearby, not in the next country. She wouldn't swear to it, but she felt like he experienced the same pull, making him want to meet her. So far, things hadn't worked out. It couldn't be the last time. Unfortunately, she was good at math. When she saw Helen, she'd already gone through three opportunities. The grocery was four. The concert might be five or five, six, and seven. If that were true, then she wouldn't have bumped into him at the restaurant, which was either six or seven. It depended on if meetings at the same place counted for one chance. At the very most, she only had one magical chance left. How to make it count? When would they meet? Apparently, Ellie knew something. She mentioned needing to tell her something in the car. A quick glance at the time on the laptop screen indicated Ellie's nap lasted over two hours. Long enough.

Guilt pinched her with its sharp, pointed fingernails as she shook her friend awake. Sure, it was bad of her, but she knew Ellie, the woman tended to forget things, which could explain why she kept going out with the same losers. Each time she managed to forget how bad they treated her and fall for the next one who came along. Ellie's eyelids fluttered open, but her eyes still held a glazed appearance.

"What?" she questioned, batting Nina's hands away. "Is it time to go to work? Did my alarm not go off?"

"No, it's Sunday. Seriously, who would wake you if your alarm didn't go off?" It certainly wouldn't be her part-time man who often never spent the night. Initially, she shared her suspicions about the possibility of Justin be married, but got such an emotional freeze out she never mentioned it again.

The petite blonde blinked, yawned, and then stretched. Her eyes scanned the room, perhaps noting the familiar landscapes purchased at the art fair they'd visited together. "Oh, I'm at your house. Why am I here?" Her brow beetled as if deep in thought.

Nina chose to say nothing, deciding to see what she actually remembered.

Her friend's face flushed red. "Oh," she gasped and held her hand to her mouth. "Tell me I didn't do what I think I did."

"You mean propositioning strange men during our champagne brunch? I would have to say you did." She pushed Ellie's legs over, which allowed her to perch on the couch.

Ellie sat up, but placed her head in her hands. "My head hurts."

"No surprise there." Pushing up from the couch, she went in search of a water bottle and pain relievers. The open floor plan of her family room and kitchen allowed her to continue the conversation as she retrieved the needed items. "Do you remember anything else?"

Turning to speak over the back of the couch, Ellie yelled as if she were yards away instead of feet. "It was only one man, not men. It was Danny Logan, not a stranger, so there."

Carrying the water bottle and medicine, she approached her friend. "How is that better?"

Ellie opened her mouth and closed it without saying anything. Her shoulders sagged, making Nina feel sorry for her friend even if she did create issues for her and Tony. After all, she couldn't blame every other failed connection on Ellie. How could she make the completely awkward situation better?

"Hey, you got to meet an old school mate?" Her forced smile probably resembled no more than a showing of teeth.

"Yeah," Ellie agreed with a total lack of enthusiasm. "Danny probably went back to his apartment and talked about what a huge ho I turned into. He even told me he had a crush on me in middle school. Then, I had to do something stupid."

Resuming her seat on the couch, Nina wondered how she could bring up the topic of Tony. Best to cut straight to the chase. Subtlety never worked when dealing with Ellie. "So did you talk about Danny's friend?"

The downward lines in her friend's face and angle of her head suggested a return to mental lecturing, the kind best done by mothers and girlfriends pretending to be your friend. Tears filled her eyes. "He must hate me. He'll never talk to me. How can I ever face him again?"

Scooting closer, she wrapped an arm around her friend's shoulders, squeezing her tight. "Honey, don't worry about it. It seems like a big deal, but nothing happened. At best, you'll meet again and laugh it off."

Her eyes took on a hopeful glint while her chin rose a few inches. "Do you really think so?"

Actually, she didn't, but the truth could be an aggressive weapon if employed ruthlessly. "Of course." She gave her an extra squeeze, hoping her friend would lie as well to her when she needed it. No one was very gracious about her soul mate discussion. Even Helen acted doubtful about the possibility of them ever meeting. Ellie wasn't exactly encouraging. Might as well forget the police officer, except he said others had reported the junk shop existing. It just winked out of existence when not needed. The desire to go back and look for it poked at her, but she knew it would do no good.

"What did you two talk about?" She'd hope her prompt might yield some info.

"What did we talk about?" Ellie repeated the question as if it might be the answer. "Not much. He called me a good girl. I remember wanting to prove otherwise, but it didn't happen." Her fingers tangled in her shoulder length hair as she twisted a strand around one finger. "Maybe school."

Great. This wasn't going anywhere. "You said in the car there was something you had to tell me."

"Yes." Ellie moved to the edge of the couch, straightening her posture. Her shoulders drooped again. "There was. It may have been significant, but I can't remember now."

That was that. Why hadn't she let Ellie talk in the car? "Don't worry, sweetie. You'll remember later." Actually, she probably wouldn't, but they both could hope.

Nina crossed her fingers, knowing her actions were mere superstitious nonsense, but some people would call the idea of a soul mate to be the same. Was it nonsense to believe one perfect person existed for her? That someone would understand her, as opposed to patronizing her by pretending to understand.

Nope, she looked at her binder on the floor. Nina had printed out all her dates and hopeful dates resulting from online dating and put them into a spreadsheet trying to find similarities. So far, nothing had worked. A company that claimed to match dozens of compatibility criteria hadn't found one date yet who *fit*.

Their criteria might be male, US citizen, and breathing, this side of fifty, two eyes, a nose, and mouth. Most were as anxious as Gavin to demonstrate they were heterosexual. If the criterion was men on the prowl for a date or a mate, then they were similar.

Sometimes she acted as if she never went out. She did, but there weren't too many repeat dates, usually by mutual decision, but mostly her. Often it didn't feel right, but once she typed her initial impressions from the date into the spreadsheet she had all the reasons it wouldn't work.

Men accused women of lying on their dating profile, but she'd swear her last four dates hadn't even read hers. That included the chain smoker who lit up five seconds into the date, despite the fact she specified no smokers in her profile. Then there was the winner who had a wedding ring tan. He tried to pass it off as being recently divorced, but she didn't buy it, especially coupled with the fact he didn't want to go anywhere public.

Men could be as clueless as women could too. "Ellie, do you remember the electrical engineer I went out with a couple of months ago?"

Her friend looked reflective for a few minutes before her eyes lit up. "The one whose hair stood straight up and you wondered if it was from being shocked too much. You obsessed on his hair, wanting to touch it."

"Thanks for making me sound so superficial." Using two fingers, she poked Ellie in the side but moved out of reach before she could get her back. "His hair wasn't what put me off though I did want to suggest some argon oil. It was the fact he talked about his ex-girlfriend and how much he loved her, but they could not be together because her ex-husband was a mobster or something."

Ellie nodded. "Sounds like a good reason to me."

"It seemed like a good reason not to date him, but he still called wondering why we couldn't go out again." She sighed and plopped back against the couch pillows.

Ellie folded her legs underneath her. "It is hard for me to keep up with your various dates. What was his reasoning for dating you while in love with another woman?"

"Same old, same old, since he can't have the woman he wants, he'd be glad to do the one he's with. When I told him no thanks, he was shocked." Her snort added to her summation of the ignorant fellow. She wondered if he lucked out with someone else. As much as she hated to admit, there were plenty of desperate women out there. Her eyes drifted to her friend, but she wiped out the thought as being uncharitable.

"First, I want you to think of yourself as the catch."

Ellie smiled at her and shook her index finger knowing she was repeating the same lecture Nina had given her numerous times, usually after a breakup. "I do. I just don't want to be second best catch. I don't want to be the woman a man settles for because he can't get what he really wants. I want to be first choice. You understand?"

By the time she'd hit thirty, most people were looking around for their second wife, which already indicated she'd not be the first choice, unless they consider their first wife a mistake, which many did.

Ellie stood, stretched her hands over her head, twisting one way, then the other. "I understand why I was so excited when Danny admitted he had a crush on me in middle school. I was his first crush, his first choice. It was thrilling for a few seconds before I realizing he now considers me a slut, an aggressive one."

The whine in her friend's voice indicating she was slipping back in maudlin. Nope, none of that. She'd just have to distract. "Can you help me pick out an outfit for the community Fourth of July party?"

Ellie followed her to her walk-in closet, throwing out suggestions. "I assume blue jean cut-offs with a halter top made out of one blue and one red bandanna is out."

"Please." She laughed at the outrageous suggestion, as intended. "I doubt we could pack the girls into two bandannas. There will be lightweight garden dresses, straw hats, and sandals. The young lesbian couple might even push it with capris."

Ellie gasped with pretend horror, holding a hand against her chest.

"A few of the residents are running for public office so they'll sport as many flags pins as possible." She giggled at the effort of last year's candidates trying to tread the line separating good taste and politics. "Andrew Stephens wore a straw boater hat with a flag hat band and was denounced as desecrating Old Glory."

"Did I thank you for inviting me to your neighborhood party? Otherwise, with no boyfriend, I'd sit at home and feel sorry for myself." She pulled out a few full-skirted dresses and held them out for perusal.

Nina didn't like any the dresses Ellie picked. She'd liked them at one time or she wouldn't have bought them, but they didn't seem right for some reason. No real reason to go all out for the party, but as her mother always reminded her, it is always wise to look your best.

A vivid tropical print with tags hanging from it tempted her. Grabbing the colorful garment, she brandished it. "What do you think? I know it is a bit loud, but it is summer. Perfect for eating chicken and potato salad, doing the meet and greet, and watching an appropriately tasteful fireworks display over the lake."

Ellie laughed. "When you put it that way, you have to wear it. There was something about your party. I just can't remember. Oh well, it must not be important."

Chapter Eight

H IS CELL PHONE'S unfamiliar alarm chirped for several minutes, barely penetrating his dreams. *There she was, smiling at him in a boat sitting on the lake. Her lips moved, but he couldn't hear what she was saying. He thought it was, "come closer," so he did. She held out her hand, welcoming him aboard her small craft. Her eyes tilted up as she smiled, saying his name. He was sure he heard his name.*

"Tony, Tony, are you going to get up? I thought the sheriff was coming promptly at eight." A series of knocks punctuated the words.

The boat drifted away, taking Nina from him. "I'm up," he shouted, mildly irritated he couldn't even finish the dream. It had the prospect of being a good one. They might have ended up falling out of the boat or at least tipping it over.

His cell phone continued to chirp until he turned it off.

A trio of knocks sounded. "Are you up? Are you going to roll over and go back to sleep?" Daniel cracked the door not waiting for a reply to his query.

Tony threw his pillow at him, but bounced off the door Daniel jerked closed. He could hear laughter on the other side.

"Sounds like you are in a good mood. I never mistook you for a morning person. What gives?"

"Possibilities. The world is full of them," Daniel said through the

90

door. His voice trailed on at the end, indicating he was walking away.

Tony knelt to pick through his suitcase for underwear. Thank goodness, this would be over soon and no more living out of a suitcase, unless his wanton ex took the furniture with her. No doubt, if she tried Mrs. Cunningham would photograph the entire event. As far as he knew, she hadn't started a neighborhood newspaper. The scrappy woman would write down the license number of the moving van and possibly try to stop it by declaring a citizen's arrest. When he got back to his house, he'd have to do something extra nice for the elderly sweetheart.

Picking out his clothes for the day, he mentally prepared himself for the coming ordeal. An Oxford shirt and khakis, no reason to look like a bum. Once in the house, he'd have access to his shorts and jeans. Having to employ a lawyer and a sheriff to get into his house was insane. His life had come to this. He didn't know anyone else who had to go through a comparable scenario, but then who would talk about it?

An abrupt knock got his attention. Before Tony even swung the door completely open, Daniel pushed a mug at him.

"Hey, buddy, I thought you could use a cup of Joe and a pep talk."

"Thanks." He accepted the cup and took a tentative sip, testing how hot it was. Not too hot, which was good, because he definitely needed the coffee. Not so much the pep talk.

"Ok, bro, I have to make this brief because the servers are down at work, which is why I am tearing out of here so early. You did nothing wrong. Sheila is the crazy chick every man encounters once in his lifetime. Hope she is your last one. Call me and let me know how it goes."

The coffee slid across his tongue black, rich, and delicious making the pep talk tolerable. He left the same blend for the elusive Mr.

Bradley. He hoped the man drank coffee. "Was that it?" Usually Daniel was much more verbose, especially on the subject of women.

"Yep." Daniel picked up a small backpack he confided he used as a man purse. It contained his babe magnet supplies including breath mints, deodorant, hairbrush and spray, lint roller, and cologne. *A man never knew when a hot woman might come across his radar* was his motto. It was best to be prepared.

The door clicked shut, leaving Tony alone with his thoughts and coffee. Alone again sounded too much like a pity party. He needed to get going so he could be alone in his own home, which shouldn't be too bad. A banana would serve as his breakfast as he drove.

At last, he was going home. It felt like years as opposed to weeks. His phone rang, which had him, patting his pockets down with one hand as he steered with the other. Having the top down made it difficult to hear, but he could tell enough it was the locksmith. "Yes, yes, ten o'clock will be okay. I'll be there. Thanks."

The locksmith's failure to show up at the original time of nine would put him behind even more. If the same man changed the locks for Sheila, he should do it free, fitting since Sheila had no proof of ownership. Who knows? She may have flashed her license or her breasts. Both would have served. Wasting a day to get back into his own house would cut into his bottom line. He had follow-up calls to make, and he had to charm Bradley. Landing the account could end up being his biggest sale this year.

The Mustang shot forward when he spotted the brown patrol car in front of his house. He pulled to the side of his driveway to allow the sheriff room to maneuver when he needed to leave. His lawyer Leon's black town car sat in front of the patrol car. The Sheriff and Leon stood under his oak tree talking. They both waved as he opened his car door.

Leon called out as he neared the two. "I bet you thought this day would never come.'

Yeah, so true. He was paying excessively much to get into his own house. He reconsidered his quip about the law working damn slow because of the County Mounty. Leon would be amused, but it was hard to know about the other man. Instead, he settled for a non-committal, "I hoped things would work out."

Leon introduced the sheriff as Officer Herman Rockwell and passed him the legal paperwork. Rockwell briefly glanced at the papers, probably figuring anyone who bothered to hire a lawyer should be on the up and up. The sheriff held out a clipboard with the household inventory attached to it. He attached a pen to the board, nodded in Tony's direction. "I have to say you are thorough in your descriptions here. Insurance companies would either love or hate you if your house burned down."

Putting his hands into his pockets, he rattled his keys. "I like to be organized. Sometimes it comes in handy."

Mrs. Cunningham came out on her porch and waved at the three of them, then ducked back into her house, probably for the camera. She might want to preserve this moment with photos. His helpful neighbor would give him a photo CD and urge him to make a screen saver with it. The kind neighbor would remind him the consequences of moving strange women into his house. Of course, he never thought Sheila would stay long since all she brought were clothes, shoes, and toiletries. He called that one wrong.

Mrs. Cunningham's door opened again, and the plump lady emerged with a plate in her hand. She stepped cautiously down the steps, moving in a sideways motion, in her orthopedic shoes and cotton housedress. Without being able to hold onto the railing, she was probably afraid she would fall. Without thinking about it, he darted across the yard to help his elderly neighbor down the stairs.

He took the plate of cookies and held out his arm to her. Together they walked toward the waiting men.

"See there, Herman, did you see what a gentleman Mr. Dante is? That's why I knew none of those horrible things the nasty Sheila creature said about him were false."

What horrible things? Was there something else besides being an abusive male? Sure, he was taller than Sheila was, but he wasn't a pit-bull of a man. A girl he once dated compared him to an Irish Setter, all flowing lines and gorgeous hair. She dropped him for a vet, which wasn't too surprising.

A red sports car turned into the drive a good thirty minutes later than the agreed upon time. Sheila slammed out of the car demonstrating her feeling about having to show up at all. A hefty, older man crawled out of the other side of the car. Was it her father? He'd never met the man.

Sheila sashayed up to the house in a pair of jean shorts, a glittery top, and red heels. Daniel would have referred to her particular ensemble a hillbilly hooker outfit, rather apt. Mrs. Cunningham ruffled up like a sitting hen. "You see, Herman. I told you she was a bad one. She's already got some other whipped man doing her fetching and carrying."

The sheriff placed a hand on the elderly woman's arm. "Aunt Adele, I need you to do me a special favor. You can stay because I know there is no way you're leaving, but you cannot say a word. It would interfere with the execution of the law."

The uniformed man stepped forward to meet Sheila and the man lumbering behind her. "Miss. Wallace, I trust you have the keys." He held out his hand.

Sheila made a show of displaying her left hand with a sizable diamond on it. "It's Mrs. Horton, now." She glanced around to make sure all eyes were on her. "My husband and I just returned from our honeymoon, in Hawaii, where I got my gorgeous tan." A swoop of her hand drew attention to her skin as if she was displaying an item for a game show.

Adele Cunningham's eyes fixed on the old man working his way up to drive. There would be no more stopping her than he could halt the spider from landing on Daniel the other day. The unsmiling officer looked a trifle anxious. "The keys, ma'am."

"Keys, oh, I lost those silly things. I just left the door open on my way to get married." She giggled like a pre-teen.

The laugh grated on Tony's nerves. Let the rest of them think she was a brainless airhead, but he knew her for the malicious bitch she was. The lost keys would have cost him the trouble of re-mastering the locks if he hadn't already planned to do that. The open house would be an excuse for missing items if someone had broken in and stole them.

Adele looked up long enough from her scrutiny of the husband to remark. "Oh, I came over and locked the door after she left. I also took photos of everything she stole while she was making a last effort to grab your speaker thing on sticks."

"My surround sound," Tony added, realizing the dear, sweet woman probably didn't know what they were.

Taking his pen, the officer wrote down a few things on his clipboard while muttering to himself. "Obstruction of justice, trespassing, theft. Okay, let's go in and see what is missing that Aunt Adele didn't manage to photograph."

Sheila aimed a glare at the elderly woman waiting patiently near the driveway, staring in the direction of the new husband. Even though it was his house and he should the others inside, he wanted to watch what Adele Cunningham would do next.

The wheezing, out of shape man tried to smile at her. "Good morning, ma'am."

Adele patted his arm. "Not so good for you. Your best bet is to run off to a doctor and get yourself tested. You see the fine, hand-some, young man standing there." She pointed in Tony's direction. "The creature you call a wife cheated on him with every male she could grab, and then she stole him half blind."

None of it sounded good. Tony was half-afraid of what he'd find when he went into the house. The man looked mildly appalled and glanced at Tony, who nodded, confirming the report.

The tiny woman pushed at the sizable man. "Go now, drive away. I happen to know she's going to the slammer. Have the marriage annulled. Tell them you were drugged. Get out while you can."

The large man flushed and immediately walked back to the car, faster than he'd come.

Inside the house, Tony found the three of them waiting for him with Sheila peeking out the window. "Where's my husband going?"

Tony watched her teeter on her too high heels, wondering what he could have found attractive about her. He remembered she was a living human who was supposed to provide companionship, greet him when he came home, and be happy to see him rather like a hairless dog. Didn't happen.

The walk through the house revealed many things were missing. The scrapbook his mother made was gone. Sheila had no use for it and probably destroyed it out of spite. He wasn't the one screwing other people in their bed. It didn't seem like she had a right to take out her spite on him. All he did was accept her cavalier treatment without too many arguments.

Leon stood by him as the sheriff handcuff the screaming, cursing and spitting woman. "You can't do this to me," she yelled, despite the fact he was doing it.

Tony wasn't sure if she was talking to him or the officer. It didn't matter. No sense of joy filled him, watching the patrol car exit his property. Guilt settled heavily on his shoulders, realizing he only had his own self to blame. After all, he let her in the door.

Leon slapped him on the back. "Cheer up, son, she's gone. It's over. You may have to declare some insurance claims and luckily you have a police record, an inventory, and detailed entries from your very helpful neighbor, which will help."

Leon was a family friend, besides being a decent lawyer. He guided them through the legal ramifications of his father's desertion when his mother had no place to turn. Fortunately, or more due to Leon's interference, his father's company didn't go after his mother for the missing funds.

Wrapping an arm around Tony's shoulder, he gave it a companionable squeeze. "Did you learn anything from this?"

"I'm a damn fool." What was he supposed to learn from it? Women were evil. He got it.

Leon released his shoulder. "Nope, you're fine. Never trust a blond." The sound of a car in the driveway caught both their attention. Seeing the shape of the locksmith's white van in the driveway, Leon moved to the door. "I'll get him to pull out so I can leave. I know you wouldn't want me to charge you for another hour."

It was hard to tell when the man was joking. "Hey, Leon, was your ex-wife a blonde?"

Leon half-turned in the doorway. "What do you think?"

The day went downhill after that which was odd because that would make the morning the highlight. After the locksmith left, he opened his dresser drawer. Well, at least the furniture was too heavy for her to move. His fingers rested on top of his folded shirt. Had anyone else opened this drawer? Better yet, had anyone worn his T-shirt? Sheila's new husband definitely wouldn't have donned it. Folded meant it was clean and unharmed.

The soft cotton shirt bore a faded logo of a bar in the Bahamas, a souvenir from a trip he and Daniel made while in college. Others headed for Florida for the spring break week of drunkenness and debauchery, but they headed for the Bahamas with Daniel's father, a pilot who had some business in the islands.

The adventure died a slow death on Cat Island, where Mr. Logan left them. The island was beautiful, its highest point, boasting a monastery they toured. They spent part of their time waiting by Mermaid Lake for the mysterious mermaid to show, which she didn't. A rupture in the ground of the island revealed the ocean. A sinkhole probably caused it. The local myths claimed a monster lived there and devoured horses. There was a singular lack of horses on the small island, which some natives pointed out proved the tale.

The thousand plus inhabitants tolerated them with laid-back charm as they enacted their version of being two wild and crazy guys. Besides working on their tans, drinking green label beer, they attempted to flirt with the two barmaids who were neither young nor attractive. The women had giggled and rolled their eyes, while neither felt charitable enough to invite them home for the night.

Mr. Logan knew what he was doing when he picked Cat Island for their adventure. On the trip back, unlike other college students who couldn't remember what they did on break or didn't dare tell their parents, Daniel retold their adventures in a lively manner, making them sound more fun than they truly were. The one thing he remembered most about the trip was the easy camaraderie between father and son. He envied it. His own father hadn't done his vanishing act yet, but he might as well for as much interaction as they had.

He rubbed the logo thinking of how long he and Daniel had been friends. His bud might be going through his lothario stage, which showed signs of waning, but he went through enough stages of his own.

A type of miasma settled on the house. The air smelt stale, which validated the story of the house being empty. Of course, if he had known the house was empty, he could have been here, not sleeping on an air mattress. Shelia ignored the inquiries made by both the deputies and his lawyer. The few calls Sheila chose to respond to were probably when she was sitting on a beach, laughing her ass off.

Sandalwood would help. Finding his incense burner and a stick, he lit it. The ninety-nine cent incense burner had not attracted her sticky fingers.

He padded through the house barefooted, inspecting each room, not sure, what he was looking for when he stepped on something sharp. Lifting his foot, he put out his hand to balance against the wall. A brush over his foot revealed a small piece of glass embedded in his heel, hard to see, but big enough to grip between his fingernails and pull out.

Holding the bloody glass up, he examined the blue shard wondering what it came from. His heart plummeted when he realized it had to be from his great grandmother's vase, one of the missing items. As the only child, his mother bequeathed to him some of the family heirlooms. The vase was a courting gift from his great-grandfather, a successful glass blower. It was rich in both sentimental and actual value. This particular shade of blue was a color developed in honor of his grandmother.

His mother was fond of telling the story. Her eyes would get glassy with the telling and sometimes she would sigh. It was obvious his mother wanted to live such a love story, but she didn't. He had never understood how his mother, who took such joy in everyone and everything, ended up with his cold, distant father.

The fact neither one of his parents had ever talked about their engagement pretty much said it all. The one wedding picture he'd seen featured the two of them looking ridiculously young and unhappy. He figured they must have had to get married since his mother was pregnant. Once he realized he'd been born too early at the grand age of thirteen, he felt some guilt at putting together two people who did not suit one another.

It would be like pairing him and Sheila. It made him shudder. Thank God, she was gone. His desire was to remove any sign of her from his house. For the most part, she left none. Her usual untidy mess of her toiletries in the second bathroom went with her. Unlike the few other women he'd been involved with, she had no desire to make her claim on his dwelling. No rearrangement of furniture, no suggestion of paint colors, no framed picture of the two of them to prominently display. No, if he'd paid more attention he would have noticed it was a non-relationship, but maybe that was what he'd wanted.

Finding the broom, he began to sweep. His goal was to get some work time in today, but he wasn't feeling it. Not only did he need to purify his house and claim it as his own once again, but also a strange upwelling of memories kept bubbling up, trapping in a moment almost forgotten. He couldn't place his finger on the why of it. At best, he decided he was at a crossroads in his life.

Moving furniture, he swept out the corners, searching for more bits of broken glass. He wondered why Sheila had done what she did. It was probably her usual modus operandus. Use a man as long as she could, then move on. Showing up with a husband in tow shocked him. He worried for a second that he'd shacked up with a married woman, making him no better than his father, the one thing he'd tried the hardest all his life to avoid.

Her husband probably already consulted with a lawyer, trying to shed himself of his larcenous wife. The big man's mistake was biting on Sheila's hook. Why did he think a woman would want to marry a man old enough to be her father? The man did all this thinking with

THE SOUL MATE SEARCH

the wrong head, obviously.

How had he fallen into Sheila's trap was the better question. The best he could remember was their meeting occurred at a party he attended. He couldn't remember whose party. It may have been at Daniel's clubhouse since Sheila didn't share any characteristics of his friends. No fashion connection demonstrated by the hillbilly hooker outfit, no common background, nothing really. She'd managed to arrange a future date with him when he was feeling maudlin.

Pushing the furniture back in place, he tried to recall the circumstances. It had been a few years after Layla broke up with him. His and Layla's relationship worked well, he thought. It was glorious compared to his and Sheila's, but he kept waiting for an inner voice to tell him this was the one. He never heard it. In the meantime, Layla happened to hear the outer voice of her future husband Jacob and decamped.

His moroseness wasn't all due to Layla leaving. Sure, the rejection stung, but it was more than that. He thought he'd nailed down the personal part of his life, only to lose it. Perhaps, he was at fault for not stepping up the relationship. Layla expected a proposal or even a suggestion they could live together, but he wasn't feeling it. His father's desertion cast a shadow on any relationship he started. Would he turn out like his father? Would he eventually destroy the relationship?

An unusual thought occurred to him making him laugh aloud. He didn't cause this last train wreck. It was all Sheila. It was probably all Sheila from the start, spotting a vulnerable man, manipulated him as much as she could until she could manipulate him no more. The thought made the incident less onerous. He wasn't at the thankful stage, but he felt good enough to call Daniel.

Chapter Nine

NINA GREETED THE sales personnel with an upraised hand and a tired smile. She didn't want to talk. All she wanted was the sanctuary of her office, where she could slip off her heels and sip a cold diet cola while shifting through the dozens of messages she knew had come in while she'd been out of the office all day.

Carlos, the general manager of the Columbus store, had some sort of mini-stroke, which put him in the hospital. Unfortunately, his assistant manager was on pregnancy leave, which left no one to fill the gap but her. She was glad she went to see Carlos in the hospital before going through his records. What she'd have to say would not have helped his recovery at all.

It was hard to tell if he was lousy at bookkeeping or whatever had caused the stroke was already at work in his brain. After a talk with her boss, they called an audit, deciding it was best to figure things out while he was in the hospital. She stopped by to see Stephanie, the assistant manager, and her new baby. Stephanie was anxious to get back to work. No reason she couldn't bring little Michel along with her since she was breastfeeding as long as the baby stayed off the sales floor. Stephanie disclosed Carlos had been preoccupied lately. It didn't mean he'd been helping himself, but rather something had dulled his typically sharp business sense.

Not finishing until late afternoon, resulted in a large pile of pink message notes littering her desk. Voice mail would be preferable, but she inherited her secretary from her boss. The dear could have retired, but preferred to work for Nina. Picking up the first message, she noted Eugenia's elegant writing. People hardly wrote in cursive anymore. The slanting letters revealed Mr. Dante, the sales rep for Allegro had called again, in person. In parenthesis, Eugenia added, (*What a looker and single too!*)

A looker. Really? What was she, a doctor? Someone easily persuaded into recommending drugs because a sexy pharmaceutical rep left free samples. No, thank you. She'd measure her suits on the quality of the merchandise and the hang of the material. She'd not be one taken in by eye candy. All the same, she wouldn't have minded meeting Mr. Dante. He did leave excellent coffee. The catalog he left behind had her intrigued too. The persistent Mr. Dante left his number. Oh well, she had to meet the man eventually, didn't she? She left his note to the side.

Halfway finished wading her way through the messages, her stomach growled. As if on cue, Eugenia walked through the door carrying a sack.

"I knew you would work through dinner, so I went out a brought you something before I left." Eugenia placed the bag on her desk. The smell of hot roast beef wafted from the sack.

"Bless you." She smiled at the woman, thinking how such actions guaranteed job security. Eugenia was old school because she actually looked after her boss.

The elegant secretary rested one hand on the door panel looking like an advertisement for a senior magazine with her French twist hairstyle and pastel suit. "Don't stay too late. Remember tomorrow is a holiday. Do not come into work."

"Yes, ma'am." She agreed with her secretary, second mother, and fashion coach. No need to mention she'd stay as long as she needed to get work done.

After wolfing down a delicious sandwich, she finished her messages. Most of the calls were follow-ups on various orders. Where were the suits, the tuxedos, the shirts, etc.? By the fifth call back and reaching voice mail, Nina realized everyone had closed for the day. Why not? It was a holiday weekend. It begged the question why she was still there.

Tomorrow was the big celebration for everyone, at least in the US. There would be plenty of cookouts, get togethers, watermelon, and pickup volleyball games. She walked through the dark showroom realizing everyone was already gone. She must not be a total ogre. After all, she did allow them to leave early for the weekend. A glance at her watch showed her it was past eight. Okay, not exactly early.

Headed to the parking lot, she waved at the mall security guard. It wasn't hard to find her car since no other cars surrounded it. A quick drive home, a glass of wine, and a soak in the tub sounded fantastic. She bought a romance novel last week she might start. It had the word soul mate in the title.

Her nose wrinkled as if she smelled something bad. She was so over that. It felt like it'd been years ago instead of a few days. Tony was delicious. Truthfully, she wouldn't mind sharing a bubble bath and a glass of wine with him, but dismissed the daydream as pure fantasy.

Her life was so hectic she didn't even have a pet, the main reason her single state. The not meeting anyone who felt right had something to do with it too. She wondered if the book would start up the longings again. She'd been too busy this week to consider a personal life. She often wondered how her employees managed a spouse and children. Pressing her fob button to unlock her car, she decided the number one thing they did was to leave work before eight. Mentally calculating the number of hours she'd put in, she tooled through the parking garage. She estimated sixty hours, and it was only a four-day week.

She almost wished there wasn't a party tomorrow. It would allow her to sleep the entire day away. Oh well, there was the weekend. Besides Ellie was so looking forward to it. Speaking of Ellie, her phone number rang, flashing up on the car's computer screen. Lowering the music first, she punched the button to answer.

Ellie started without the usual hello. "Are you excited or what?"

Her friend's enthusiasm was another reason she couldn't cancel. "Yippee, woo-hoo." She tried to match Ellie's attitude, but failed miserably, sounding more like a wind-up toy slowing down.

"You need to work on that. What time do you want me over?"

The party wasn't until two, which would allow her plenty of sleeping time. "One."

"Get real. We need to glam up to get ready for our big chance at romance. I'll be there at ten."

Ouch. It would cut into her sleeping plans. She might have to wake up and get dressed before ten. "Sweetie, I am sorry to disappoint you, but I seriously doubt there will be very little romance in the works tomorrow. Most of my neighbors are couples. Those who aren't are women who won the house in the divorce battle."

Ellie's laugh reflected a light-heartedness reflective of a kid on a Christmas Eve. "Nina, Nina, you are overlooking the possibilities. Your neighbors will invite guests, cousins, brothers, and co-workers."

"Their wives and their screaming children," she added, knowing Ellie probably stuck out her tongue at the comment.

"Then there's the firemen, the off-duty policeman hired for crowd control, even the politicians. They can't all be married."

"I am worried about you, friend. You mentioned politician under the heading of available men. You're welcome to comb through all my online dating profiles. I haven't glanced at them in three weeks. Last time I did was only to get Gavin's phone number. You remember how that worked out."

"He was nervous," Ellie explained with a giggle, making Nina realize her friend wasn't serious.

"If that was nervous, I'll pass on confident. Besides, think how excited my matches would be to get a petite blonde instead a full figured Italian gal." She imagined her potential dates smiling at the switch.

"Nina, will you stop it? You have no clue how gorgeous you are. Men's eyes follow you every time you stride through the room with your haughty nose in the air."

Playfully, she put a nose in the air. "I do not have my nose stuck in the air." She shook her head even though Ellie couldn't see it. There was nothing snooty about her. She was one of the most down to earth people she knew.

Her friend's sigh filled the car. "I should have known you'd take it that way. It's not a bad thing. It gives you an aloof, untouchable aspect, the opposite of most women who shove out the girls as a welcome mat. I know you're shy, but men see you as unobtainable. You are the distant ice queen. Being perverse creatures, men preferred the aloof female. Even your failure to make second dates with your online hopefuls just reinforces the image. Do the guys you go out with ever call you?"

"They do. You know they do, but I don't have time to waste on dates with no potential. Sometimes I wish they wouldn't call, forcing me to find creative excuses to sound like I am not rejecting them."

"Lying is what you're doing. Why don't you look at the next man you meet as fun, not relationship material, but a good time? Men do it all the time. That's going to be my plan tomorrow. I am going to have a good time."

Nina winced, thinking of her friend flirting with the problem men in the neighborhood. There were a few. "Can I steer you away from the few major sleazes?"

"That's what friends are for." Ellie breezily commented.

Nina tried to drag up memories of various men in the community, but she wasn't the best source, since all she did was drive into her garage. Her few interactions were limited to catching a couple of neighbors allowing their dogs to crap in her yard, which was against the covenant she pointed out as they hustled their purebred canine away from her property. A gossipy woman in the health club felt obligated to point out the available men and warning against some of them. She wondered at the time if the woman had dated the men. Was her warning to discourage her from pursuing men she had her eye on? It was a moot point. She could no more strike up a conversation with a stranger than she could make a cold call, which explained her career in management and acquisition.

The memories of red-faced men in athletic clothing trying to lift weights too heavy for their ability, while retaining a certain amount of savoir-faire while aware women were staring, came to mind, but it didn't help much. The only way she'd recognize them was if they donned a sweatband and were sweaty and flushed. Since it was July, the sweaty and flushed part might not be too difficult. As for the truthfulness of her informer, who knew?

"Okay, I'll see you tomorrow. Bring your bikini and clothes to stay overnight. I hope I'll remember the men you should avoid. I may not, but I will do my best. I'll see you tomorrow. Bye."

The gate swung open on her number completion, allowing her to enter. A bath was her top priority with the wine being second. A possible dip in the community pool meant she's have to do a full shave instead of her work shave, which ended somewhere above her knees. Oh well, it would make Ellie happy.

She entered her silent home, wishing she had some sort of welcome. Even though she disliked cats, a furry feline meowing its welcome would have been preferable to the emptiness. On the other hand, it might be complaining, nagging at her in cat language for food and a clean cat box, which explained why she didn't have a cat. Since it was a smart house, she could program music to turn on ten minutes before her arrival, but she didn't. Somehow, she viewed it as being more pitiful than the silent residence. It indicated a pretense as if she were attempting to fool herself.

Three steps into the house and she turned on the music she'd earlier ridiculed herself for considering. It was okay if she turned it on, she assured herself. After finding the South African wine, she favored, she filled up a balloon shaped goblet as far she could to the rim. Taking a sip to lower the level, the crisp flavor of bottled sunlight and joy rolled across her tongue, enlivening it. If she went into advertising instead of men's suits, her commercial for the wine would feature a wildflower-strewn field with butterflies dancing across the screen. A couple would enter the scene carrying a picnic basket and holding hands. The woman would have on a summery dress, and her hair would be loose, rippling in the breeze. The man would wear a white Havana shirt. She smiled at the image, thinking they would stop, kiss, spread a tablecloth on the ground, open up the wine, and toast one another with glass goblets they brought for their romantic tryst.

Twisting the tub handles, she started the water. Strange the man in her ad looked a great deal like Tony, even down to his glasses, and the woman was a spitting image of herself. She hadn't put 'the search' behind her. That's why she needed to find the book. Better to read about someone else's idea of romance than to dwell on something that wasn't going to happen. The book sat her in the bedside drawer underneath Bob. Yep, it was the sum total of her love life, a paperback, and battery-powered boyfriend.

Picking up a container of bath salts, she shook some into the water releasing a gardenia scent. Gavin was more than willing to be her real life boy toy. Only problem was he wasn't exactly the model she wanted. In most ways, he was an average fellow, although a little better than most. It was more an issue of not fitting together, despite Gavin's attempt to prove he did fit. It was like putting a puzzle together, sometimes you could force the pieces together, but it didn't mean they actually belonged together.

The water was at the depth she wanted, and she twisted the faucet off. She draped her clothes across the towel rack. When it came to throwing clothes on the floor, she drew the line at custom suits. Andy, their veteran tailor, stitched up a few custom suits for her out of the fabric they used for their men's suits. He usually started with a forty jacket to put in the appropriate darts for her bosom, but he was on his own when it came to the skirt. She shed her lavender lace lingerie and pinned up her hair before stepping into the water.

The water felt wonderful. Most people might avoid a hot bath in the summer, but they hadn't spent a long week in heels either. It would have been easier to walk around in flats and pants and be as androgynous as most women in business. She'd cut off her thick waves for a short style, but then she'd be giving away her feminine power according to her mother, Carlotta. *"God made you a woman for a reason."* She could hear her mother's voice in her head. *"Too many women try to be men,"* her mother would continue with her favorite lecture. She could almost repeat the lecture word by word. As a kid, she may have laughed at it, but her mother lived it. Her father adored his wife, rushing to open doors and escorting her around as if they were courting.

Men responded to her mother. They were not actually flirtatious, although a few flirted lightly, knowing nothing would come of it.

Instead, it was as if her presence reminding them they were men as opposed to asexual clones. They often smiled at her as they held the door open for her. Ellie was willing to bet her mother may have never actually pumped gas until her father died. Even now, she doubted she did, since she went to the only service station in the city that still pumped gas and washed windows.

Carlotta was a beautiful woman, not stick thin by any means. Still, even at sixty, she turned masculine heads. It was an attitude. Her mother knew her feminine power and wielded it like a whip. Last time she visited home, her mother's friends commented on how much she looked like a younger version of her mother. The same women would elaborate on how many hearts she must break, including her mother's because she hadn't provided a single grand-child. She always pointed out her brother, Joseph, made up for her lack with his four children.

How odd. She never considered herself like her mother. Did she want to be like her mother? She certainly wouldn't mind being adored. Laying her damp hand on the book, she stared at the couple on the cover. They were carrying a picnic basket and he was wearing a Havana shirt. How weird was that? She blinked, and the cover morphed back into a Regency cover of a man pushing a woman on a swing. She must be more exhausted than she realized.

Placing the book on the tub sill, she leaned back against the end and closed her eyes. A little rest might help. Even with her eyes closed, she saw him smiling at her, beckoning. His smile was open and inviting. The ivory shirt showed up well against his tanned skin. His eyes sparkled with mischief behind his glasses. His hair, all loose curls, layered to hug his skill, inviting her fingers to touch.

"What are you waiting for?" his lips seem to say. It was easy for him to say since they'd never been introduced.

What was she waiting for? "You, of course." Her words echoed in the tiled bathroom making her feel foolish.

Still, if she ran into the man again, she'd make a definite impression, certain it would technically be her last time. She wasn't sure how the soul mate concept worked. She assumed if they met, connected, they would continue to see one another. Wouldn't each meeting count as a chance? If that were the case, then seven would be a very paltry number. If she saw Tony tomorrow, she vowed to latch onto him and create a memorable day. Her eyelids fluttered open with a crazy plan. Holding the book in one hand and her wine glass with another, she vowed to the listening air. "July Forth will be the day, my soul mate and I become one."

Something shivered in the air, almost as if something brushed her face. It just showed her how tired she was. She'd better exfoliate and shave before she fell asleep in the tub. In less than ten minutes, she found herself in bed. Sleep, she would welcome it. Plumping up her feather pillow, her eyes flickered close. All she needed to do was avoid any dream about plucking out eyeballs and sharing them.

Why did she have to think of that? Her eyes snapped open in the dark bedroom. Music played in the living room since she forgot to turn it off. The sensible thing would be to get up and turn off the music. Yep, sensible, she always made the practical choice. Not tonight, though, she was tired. What would it hurt if it stayed on? Didn't she pay the bills? Tonight, she'd have an easy listening soundtrack to her dreams.

The mist broke, exposing a wooden rowboat. Nina sat in the non-moving boat tied to the lakeside dock. The oars were in the locks, but she'd never rowed a boat in her life, and she wasn't worried. He'd come, she knew he would. Part of her knew she was dreaming, noting she wore the dress she'd picked out for the Fourth. It looked good on her.

The sound of a brass band playing patriotic songs carried well across the water. Of course, they'd have a brass band. Their latest political hopeful, probably arranged it. Children laughed and darted through the willows edging the waters. She could hear mothers calling out half-hearted instruction about more sunscreen and staying away from the water. A few shrieks and splashes alerted her not all followed the directives. The scent of hamburgers and hot dogs, cooking rode the breeze along with the sounds.

A pleasant sense of anticipation filled her as she looked in the direction of the shore. He was coming soon. She could feel it. The certainty of his arrival settled on her, bringing with it a sense of peace. Her enjoyment of the sun warming her back faded as she saw him. He sauntered through the trees wearing a white Havana shirt paired with beige linen trousers. Ah, she did love a man with a sense of fashion. Her business eye judged the quality of the material and the drape, all good.

His lips kicked up when he caught sight of her in the boat. He held his hand up in greeting as he came closer. "There's my soul mate. You made me search for you."

She laughed with absolute joy. He was here. All was right with her world. "I was waiting for you. What took you so long to find me? So many chances and for basic purposes, so close together. Sometimes, we were only inches from one another."

He jogged the last few steps to the dock. "Inches often can be further apart than most suspect." He crouched to untie the boat.

Part of her wanted to caution against untying it before he stepped in. A voice called his name causing him to turn and drop the rope. The boat drifted amazingly fast, for what was normally a sluggish current. "Tony," she called out in her distress.

His face filled with horror as she gradually moved away from him. The lake wasn't big, her logical side reminded. She would quickly end up on the other side where they'd meet again. She could also try using the oars. The reason they were there. The dream didn't listen. It was all *symbolic. Her last chance was vanishing.*

She woke up abruptly, hearing music in the dark, someone singing about if he died first he'd wait at Heaven's gate for his soul mate. It was exactly what she didn't need to hear while she shivered from the aftereffects of the realistic dream.

Sleep didn't come easy. Tossing and turning accompanied her thoughts of missed chances, mystical happenings, and soul mates kept her from falling back to sleep easily. She wished Nona Caprice were here. Her grandmother died before her father, making the last eighteen months hard. If she wanted to ask about magical wishes, dreams, or even fairies, Nona Caprice was her go-to person. Even her name meant whimsical and fanciful. What advice would her grandmother give her?

The opinionated woman had a strong streak of practicality too. Her advice might be to clasp a virile man to her bosom while she could get the most enjoyment out of it. Wait too long and she might not be able to do half the things she'd dreamed of doing. It wasn't bad advice even if she imagined it herself. It was time to take chances and do things she wanted to do.

No sleep tonight unless she resorted to chemical help. She debated having dark circles under her eyes and little energy compared to looking rested on the morrow. Chemicals it was. On her way to the kitchen, she turned off the stereo. Who needed depressing songs? Not her, if she couldn't have an actual living, breathing man, then what good was a soul mate?

On the way to the kitchen, she thought she smelled hamburgers cooking. Talk about your vivid dreams. Two sleeping pills later, she found herself slipping into a dreamless sleep, only to be awakened the next morning by some lunatic playing a tune with her doorbell. Who would do such a thing in the middle of night? Her hand landed on her phone with her eyes still closed. Should she call the community security or the regular police? The sound of her garage door opening replaced her doorbell serenade. Her eyelids snapped open. "What the?"

Sunlight streamed in through the blinds, indicating it was way past dawn. Frozen in fear, she listened to her garage door open. Was this the end? There was so much left she wanted to do. She never made it to Italy, to Grandma Caprice's birthplace. Wait, who had the code to her garage? Possibly Neighborhood Security and... the kitchen door opened, letting her home invader in.

"Don't tell me you're still in bed. What did you do last night, tie one on?" Ellie's familiar voice came closer.

Nina smiled in relief. Life would go on at least a little longer. The sleeping pills left her groggy and slow to respond.

A spritely knock sounded on her door similar to the doorbell tune. "Is everyone decent inside or will I find your nude body underneath four cabana boys?"

"I wish." Nina made her lips form the words, although they sounded peculiar to her own ears.

Ellie walked in with a troubled expression. "You aren't sick, are you?" She drew closer and perched on the edge of the bed.

Nina opened her mouth to speak, but a yawn came out instead. "Sorry, I meant to say no. Took two sleeping pills last night when I couldn't sleep, and I didn't wake up until you came in. Thought you were some serial killer coming to kill me."

"There's a cheerful thought." Ellie peeled back the end of the comforter to get to Nina's feet. Taking a forefinger and thumb, she pinched Nina's instep.

"Hey, what was that for?" Pulling her foot back under the covers, she directed a glare at her friend.

Giggling, Ellie pulled up the covers again to reach for the other foot. "I just want to get you fully awake. Big day remember. It is our fun day. I show up, and you are still in bed." She bounced on the bed a little.

"I'm up, all right," Nina rolled to the other side of the bed to avoid her friend's helpful pinches. Standing, she stretched. "Maybe I should hit the shower to awaken fully."

Her friend began smoothing out the bedcovers and plumping the pillows.

"What are you doing?" She watched Ellie with an amused glance. Housekeeping wasn't in her friend's skill set. Her abode resembled a picked over yard sale. It always amazed her how Ellie could find anything in the chaos.

Delivering a final pat to the bed, she turned to grin. "Go get clean up. I'll do some light housekeeping. You want your home to be at its best for what promises to be an enchanted evening."

"Enchanted evening? Are you my fairy godmother?" She chuckled at her own joke.

Using the skirt of her sundress, Ellie tried to dust the dresser without much success. "Do you have a feather duster or something? Something magic is in the air. Surely you feel it."

She had felt something last night. "I think you're right." Perhaps it would be an enchanted evening. She left her friend dusting with a pair of discarded stockings that never reached the hamper from the day before.

Chapter Ten

I F IT WASN'T a holiday and everyone he needed to talk to had taken the day off, Tony might have considered going into work. Recovering his home, gobbled up his Monday. On Tuesday, he had to swear out charges on Sheila. He should have done that while the sheriff was at his house. He had managed to get a little work done despite his wasted time downtown. Only two work days left and he'd still had no luck catching up with Bradley. It was too bad he'd be out of town most of the next week.

Today, with most of his customers already started their holiday weekend, would be a good day to work on sales projections along with actual orders that needed analyzing. His numbers might humble him. They'd certainly prevent him from getting salesperson of the year as he did the previous three years. Wasting a day was frustrating when he'd only had a two and a half day work week so far. Still, he had customers in other countries. It might be a good time to confer with them. Glancing at his watch, he decided to call the British buyers. Often, he just shot the breeze with them so when he did have something to sell, they'd be more likely to buy from him as opposed to a person who just wanted to move merchandise. Truthfully, he considered the British buyers, Christian and Preston, friends.

A flurry of chiming notes indicated the doorbell. Shouldn't be any deliveries, but Mrs. Cunningham might feel obligated to invite the lonely bachelor over for a meal. Instead, Daniel stood there. His eyes swept over a color-coordinated polo and Bermuda shorts. His friend sported a grin and a mischievous look.

"Don't tell me you are wearing that?" His friend gave his faded jeans and T-shirt a disdainful look.

Who elected him as the fashion police? "Why should it matter what I wear?" He backed up, making space. Why was he here? Common courtesy dictated conversation, even if the man did delay his overseas calls. Part of him welcomed the diversion. As a man, he tried not to make a big deal out of holidays, even though his mother always did. He even called his mother last night to see what she was up to today and found her to be reticent. Not wanting to talk about her plans, only declining a meeting with him by claiming a previous engagement.

Daniel walked around him slowly, clicking his tongue. "I did expect better of you. An excellent opportunity is at your feet, and this is what you wear. Despite having the gate code, I doubt we'll be let in."

"What are you talking about?"

Daniel moved on from inspecting his wardrobe to scrutinizing his shelves. "Remember the Fourth of July party in Nina's gated community. Don't tell me you forgot?"

Gesturing to the house, he arched his eyebrow for emphasis as he spoke. "In case, you forgot I was doing some major legal maneuvering to get back into my own house. I forgot."

Picking up a small ornamental globe, Daniel held it up, inspecting it. "I know some things are missing, but I would be hard-pressed to tell you what. You told me she grabbed as much as she could before she drove off to her wedding."

Shrugging his shoulders, he tried to find humor in the situation that was still rather raw. "I think she picked through my stuff and helped herself to several wedding and goodbye presents."

Daniel wrinkled his nose. "Hey, I know it is bad taste asking and all, but the guy you caught her with, was he the one she ended up marrying?"

Walking up to his friend, he put his hand on his chest and shoved. "Yes, it's very bad taste. No, not the same guy. The man she drove here with on Monday would have had a heart attack when I came busting in. Mrs. Cunningham assures me I surprised a married man. Don't know how she knows, but oddly, I do not doubt her. I always want that woman on my side."

Daniel held up a stick with a small rock attached to it. "I see she didn't take your weather tree. When are you going to get dressed? There is a difference between being fashionably late and missing out on all the food." He replaced the weather tree carefully, centering it on the shelf.

Shaking his head at the antics, he grinned, knowing Daniel was secretly pleased he kept the tree. As cub scouts, they both went to summer camp together. His weather tree had been the victim of a bully who was also the scoutmaster's son. Looking back, Tony realized it would have been easy to assemble another tree. At the time, he couldn't get past Thad, the bully, destroying his for no other reason than he could. Daniel, seeing his face pucker up immediately, had shoved his tree into his hands, helping him save face in front of the thug. Tears would have pleased Thad. He kept the tree to remind him that no matter how he might act, underneath the surface, Daniel was a person he could depend on. "Now I remember the picnic. Are we really going with an invitation delivered by a drunk female? The gate code is probably wrong too."

"Nope. She repeated it rapidly like it was something she knew without even thinking about it. As for the invite..." He stopped to smirk. "She's probably forgotten about it. Tried to wipe the incident from her mind, but it doesn't mean I've forgotten."

The plan had disaster written all over it, even though he would like another opportunity to talk to Nina. He'd had longer and more meaningful conversations with his neighbor. Rubbing his open palm over his stubbly face, he considered the appropriate actions. "I don't know. She probably doesn't want to see you."

Daniel sucked in his lips, an old habit, which relayed his uncertainty. "True, true, but I want to see her. Damn it, man, she is the only female who liked my geeky self. She had a crush on me. I am unwilling to let it go. What if you knew there was someone out there perfect for you? In the beginning things didn't work out as well as you might like, but you knew if you persevered you'd hit pay dirt? Wouldn't you persevere?"

Persevere. Did he ever persevere in the name of romance? In business, he had the stubbornness of a mule and the tenacity of a pit bull. "I hate it when you're right." He pretended to glower at his friend before heading off to shave.

As he lathered up his face, he heard Daniel's footstep. "Do you want me to pick out your clothes?"

Sticking his lathered face out the bathroom door, he said, "Seriously, did you forget what I do for a living? I got this."

As his razor cut through the shaving cream, he contemplated what he should wear. Not a polo and Bermudas. Too cliché, something simple, lightweight, and unconstructed. Linen pants and a Havana shirt would work. No toe cleavage, either. Most men's feet were not attractive. Did Daniel have on sandals? Oh well, too late to mention it. Besides, he wouldn't take his fashion advice well.

A blue bottle of high-end cologne beckoned on the shelf. He paid plenty for the spicy scent, probably influenced by the advertisement featuring an adventurous man who eventually allows the hot chick to catch him. He'd stopped wearing it. He never landed any hot babes with it, and a few of his clients were fussy about smells. He held the bottle up to the light, causing the contents to list to one side. To use it would signal some level of belief he could entice Nina close enough to smell it. He put the bottle back on the shelf but didn't lose his grasp on it. What was so wrong about hope? He twisted off the lid and splashed some on his hand, then distributed it to his neck and chest.

A little sparkle glistened in the air, probably resulting from the strong light coming in through the bathroom window and bouncing off the mirror. Sunlight from that angle indicated the sun was climbing to its apex right above his house, meaning it was at least noon. Running damp fingers through his hair, he noticed one side was flatter than the other was. It was from sleeping on it, but he doubted he had time to wet it down and start again. With traffic, it might take them forty-five minutes or more to make it to the celebration. A liberal application of hair gel allowed him to puff up his flat side.

Part of him ridiculed his intensive grooming efforts, but another part wanting the attention. What was wrong with looking well groomed? Women thought it was important. Thankfully, Daniel had no clue how much work he put into his appearance. It might be hard for him not to tease.

It only took him a few minutes to don his clothing and slip into his shoes. Catching a glance of himself, he thought he looked casual without having fussed too much. Other men may know he had spent too much time in front of the mirror, but their opinions didn't matter. He opened his door, almost ready to leave, but decided to grab one more item from his dresser drawer. Daniel stood in the doorway, hooking his hand on the top edge of the door.

Angling his head toward the box springs with a comforter spread across it, he said, "I see you got rid of your mattress."

"Yep, it's in the garage. I couldn't sleep on it. When I get a new one, the delivery men will haul off the old. Enough. I'm ready to indulge in Fourth of July festivities, gated community style."

His friend slapped him on the back. "Then let's go bro. I think we should take my car."

The babe sedan. Better yet, it was a mint green. It had to be a custom paint job. No self-respecting German car company would ever paint a car that color. Daniel bought it used, which explained the color. For reasons unknown, he considered it a babe mobile. So far, it hadn't lived up to its title. Probably because every woman who saw it realized it was a chick car and assumed the male driver was gay, taken, or both.

"Okay." He concurred without a fuss because he didn't want to explain his reasoning. Two men dressed as if they could appear on a cover of man's fashion layout in a mint green sedan did not shout macho. His goal was to get out of the car as soon as possible, which was dependent on them actually getting through the gate.

Daniel, wired to the max, talked the entire trip, hardly waiting for a reply. "Can you believe it? Ellie and me running into each other. What are the odds?"

Before Tony could point out the odds were good since they both continued to reside in the same area and were of similar age, his friend launched into another middle school recollection. Was he thirteen? Hadn't he heard this story before, over twenty years ago? Why didn't he and Nina ever meet earlier?

Wait, they did, several times in fact, many more than he realized. Who knew when they passed each other, but failed to look? A couple of years ago, when he was at the outside concert with Layla, Nina could have been there with date or husband. There was no reason to think she was available. The two of them had never been together long enough for him to check out her left hand. His mood worsened, causing him to snarl at Daniel's light-hearted banner.

"Who pissed in your cornflakes? Wait, you didn't have breakfast. Could be the problem."

Daniel continued to drive with one arm out the window and a goofy expression, announcing his belief that life was good. Too bad, Tony couldn't be as sure. Still, if Nina were married, she wouldn't be fending off her amorous men in the parking lot. If the man had any type of attachment, he wouldn't have been forcing his campaign. Life was good, at least for today.

The car idled about a foot away from the security keypad. Not far enough to get out and use it, but too far to reach it quickly. Twisting his upper body half through the open window, Daniel punched in the code. Tony slumped in his seat and kept his eyes down as if he found his cuticles interesting. Wonder of wonders, the gates swung open.

Large stone houses with ornate arches and canopies stretched over the driveways to prevent anyone exiting their cars while open to the elements. It reminded him of a funeral home, but knew the home-owners would not appreciate such a comparison. A few homes, even had a few Corinthian columns in the yard as if their house was part of a Grecian temple or an English folly. Obviously good taste was not a requirement to live in this neighborhood. A few homes boasted bushes trained and trimmed into the shape of vases and flowers. Actual flowers with color and fragrance were notable by their absence.

The smell of hamburgers cooking rode the air, along with voices and the robust music of a brass band. An American flag the size of a large car rippled in the wind close to the lake. Pointing to the flag, he said. "Over there is where everything is happening. There is bound to be some type of parking lot. We can park and scout out the premises."

"Scout out the premises." Daniel repeated his words with enthusiasm. "Sounds like we're on a top secret mission."

It was a mission all right, to get his friend connected to his middle school sweetie with no guarantees of happiness after they met. The rest was up to Daniel, who Tony sincerely hoped had given up on his lounge lizard ways. No sober woman ever fell for those. Of course, he didn't know if the much talked about Ellie would be sober, but he was willing to bet she would.

His fingers smoothed over the box in his pocket, wondering what made him bring it. He could leave in the car for safekeeping, but it had very little monetary value. It was another family heirloom passed through generations. Apparently, his great grandfather gave it to his great grandmother, calling her his true love, and the necklace was proof of it. Somehow, a tradition popped up when the son of the family gave it to his significant other. His mother had no brothers, so the necklace was hers to pass on to her son.

The box traveled with him wherever he moved since he was twenty. It was with him when he carried Nina's box to her room, although not on him, but in his dorm room. For almost twenty years, he had carried it. Amazing Sheila hadn't made off with it, but she didn't spend any time in his underwear drawer. He couldn't picture her folding his boxer briefs and putting them away. He wasn't even sure he'd seen her do laundry. Realistically, she must have, but never in his presence.

Looking back, he'd accepted, they were friends with benefits without even the friend's part. He never wanted to consider himself that crude. The benefits disappeared over time. It was difficult to say when, but probably months ago. Initially, he inquired when she was going to move every month, but the fit she threw made him dial back his questions. In the end, he thought it would end like this. Yep, he could have lived without the drama.

All he needed to have done was push her out. If push came to shove, he could have changed the locks. He did nothing because he really didn't want to deal with her theatrics. He tried to freeze her out by not being romantic or thoughtful, thinking a lack of interest would get her going, but it hadn't. He attempted to shake her down for rent and utilities. Sheila only made excuses why she couldn't pay. She'd promise to pay, and then swear something had happened that she couldn't.

At no time did he consider giving the necklace to Sheila, Layla, or even Veronica, his first love. Veronica procured the prize as best girlfriend until she traveled to Europe and decided a man with an accent triumphed every time. He patted his box, realizing the urge to grab it came out of nowhere. No sooner had he placed it in his pocket than a sense of rightness fell upon it, which was weird in itself with the way everything had gone wrong lately.

Parking the car in a side lot, hidden by trees, Daniel pocketed the keys and opened the car door. "Here goes nothing. Wait." He reached for a small breath spray cylinder, pumping it once in his mouth, and then slipping it into his shorts' pocket.

Grateful for his hidden parking space, Tony joined him on the blacktop. "I think we should wander around and see if we see them."

Daniel shifted his feet and jingled the keys in his pocket. "It's a workable idea, but what if someone asks us why we're here. What are we going to say?"

Daniel's confidence stayed behind in the car when confronted with the reality of meeting the female he'd talked about non-stop for a week. Thankfully, Tony's move on Monday kept most of his friend's reminiscing about his middle school crush at a minimum, but it didn't save him from all of it. Seeing Daniel's anxiety, he did his best to relieve it.

"No worries, bro." He nudged his friend with his elbow, while angling his head toward the people milling on the perfectly land-scaped commons in the distance. "These people believe themselves too well-bred to ask. They will assume we are expensive gigolos here to service the women of the community. Naturally, they can't ask what woman we are servicing. Business code and all that." He winked, seeing Daniel enjoyed the idea of being a gigolo. Tony imagined he would.

His confidence restored, Daniel gestured in the direction of the structure supporting the oversized flag. "Let's head on over to the gazebo. I think the food and music are located there."

The noise grew louder as they grew closer, confirming Daniel's deduction. People huddled in small groups on the grassy banks of the small lake. Some glanced their way. Most men immediately broke eye contract, demonstrating they did not consider them worthy of a lengthy appraisal. Such an appraisal might bring their orientation into question. Some of the women didn't worry about checking them out thoroughly, despite standing beside their husbands.

A woman detached herself from a group and approached them with a Botox smile welded into place. "Good afternoon," she drawled holding out her hand to Tony. "I'm Pamela Plastich. You are?"

Their first test—already. Clasping her hand firmly he gave his best client-pleasing smile, guaranteed to assure the client he was not only pleased to make his acquaintance, but he was trustworthy, knowledgeable, leaving the client in a bit of awe of such a fashion giant. The woman fluttered her eyelashes, which may have been as much expression as she could manufacture. Apparently, his professional mien worked well on non-clients too. All this time he'd had a formidable weapon in his dating arsenal he had never used.

"Hi, I'm Tony Dante, and this is Daniel Logan." He angled his head in Daniel's direction.

Daniel's outstretched hand and smile demonstrated his readiness.

She released Tony's hand to take Daniel's. "Dante and Logan sound like actor names. You two are certainly handsome enough to be actors or male models."

Daniel colored under the heavy-handed flattery. "Thank you, m…" He stumbled on the word, but managed to change it in time. "Pamela."

She gave a playful tap to Daniel's shoulder after he released her hand. "All my friends call me Pammy. You can call me Pammy."

Daniel sent a panicked look over the woman's head, which Tony Reid. "Well, Pammy," Tony said, earning a narrowed eyed look, due to the fact she didn't invite him to call her Pammy. "We are here to meet friends, so we need to go. Great meeting you."

Daniel walked away, anxious to escape the randy female. Probably the first time he'd been on the other end of the stick. She took a few rapid steps after him and called out. "Who are your friends? I may know them."

Daniel's eyes took on a haunted look, well aware a semi named Pammy might decorate her grill with his carcass in mere seconds.

Tony threw over his shoulder. "It would be indiscreet to mention their names."

Daniel whispered. "Indiscreet. That was good. I wish I thought of it."

"I'm discovering the game of sexual attraction is very similar to a business. The same words and actions work in both." He mentally congratulated himself until Pammy managed to catch up with them.

"You're Robert and Leonard's guests. I should have known." After delivering her volley, she sailed past the men.

Daniel blanched at the implications. "Shouldn't we correct her assumptions?"

"Absolutely not. It gives us a reason for being here. Coming from Pammy's mouth makes it more believable. Let's get something to eat.

It has been at least twelve hours since I had real food."

Rubbing his hands together in anticipation, he said, "I can wait to sink my teeth into some mustard potato salad, baked beans, and charred dogs."

As they drew closer to the gazebo, he spotted two men attired in aprons and chef hats staffing the grill. Other white smocked employees stood behind the tables decorated with red, white, and blue bunting. One female employee flashed a professional smile that didn't reach her eyes as she handed them the china plates clutched in her latex-gloved hands. "Vegan or carnivore?" she asked.

His brows went up at the question. Was he a grazer or a meat eater?

Noting his confusion, she explained. "We have vegan sausage and caramelized onion, lettuce and tomato sandwiches on unseeded peasant bread for the non-meat eaters. For the carnivores," she said with a grimace, demonstrating her feeling on the matter, "Smoky Chipotle Chicken burgers and Mesquite Bison Burger. Which would you like?"

"Bison," Tony stated, since it sounded the most like hamburger. Daniel copied his choice.

The employee turned to speak to the fellow at the grill. "Two on the range, flesh eaters."

While Daniel choked, Tony directed an annoyed glance at the young employee.

Seeing his look, she pleaded. "Don't report me. I need this job."

"You don't act like you need it," he muttered more to himself than to her.

Her lips thinned into a stubborn line, showing why she might have issues with keeping a job. "You're the first people that actually paid attention to me. Trust me. I've been saying similar stuff all day."

"Keep in mind, the next person who really listens to you may have paid for this expensive spread. Sometimes it just makes sense to keep your opinions to yourself." He cautioned her, well aware he'd learn the lesson at a young age with his own father. At the time, he thought he had the meanest father in the world, but he did teach him one useful skill.

"I'll remember," the girl begrudgingly assured him. "Do you need me to dip your cold foods?"

"Amazingly, we might be able to do it on our own." He reached for the spoon planted in the quesadilla salad.

"You'd be the first," she muttered low.

He tapped the spoon against his plate. "I can still hear you."

Daniel ignored the sullen teen to point out the various labels standing in front of each dish. "There's Maple Olive Oil Apple Chips. Hello? Where are the regular potato chips?" Despite his grumbling, he still took a hand full. The woman in front of him stared at the spoon in the chip bowl.

"Hey, look! There's zucchini slaw and spiced tomato salad." Tony's attempt to bolster his companion's food attitude may have experienced some success, especially after spotting the chocolate chip and pecan cookies.

The burger chef held a bison burger on his spatula. "Do you want this with cheese?"

He nodded, not wanting to get into another discussion with the catering staff.

Another employee waited nearby to slap the cheese on the burger. Gesturing to a large tray of assorted cheeses he asked, "Do you want Gouda, smoked Gouda, provolone, cheddar, Edam…?"

"Cheddar." His reply stopped the employee from listing the dozen or more other cheeses. The plated burger came down the line to another employee who stood behind various types of buns with labels on each. The label on first one read Honey Wheat.

"Honey wheat," he said before she could ask.

They carried their plates to a small table with an umbrella and patriotic tablecloth. Pulling out the white plastic rental chairs, they both sat. Daniel looked at the food, then at him. "Who knew getting food at a picnic involved so many decisions. Usually, I just got whatever there was and liked it."

Another employee appeared at their table asking what they would like to drink, listing the wines and micro brews appropriate for their food. Danny seemed to consider the alcohol, which would be a bad deal for the romantically-challenged man.

Tony held up two fingers. "Ice tea."

The server sighed a little before launching into the list. "Do you want black tea sweetened or unsweetened, decaf black, herbal mint, lemonade and tea mixed, raspberry tea sweetened?"

"Black sweet tea," he said, the words coming out in a terse tone, overwhelmed by all his choices, hoping they had plain sweet tea.

Daniel held up a finger for attention. The waiter addressed him. "Yes, sir?"

"Is your tea free trade? I'm not sure I could drink anything that wasn't." Daniel acted distressed, causing the waiter to react equally.

"Oh, no, sir, we would never serve anything that wasn't free trade."

Tony kicked him under the table. At the rate they were going, he'd never get anything to drink.

Daniel nodded at the waiter. "Splendid. That sounds acceptable." The waiter disappeared to get their tea.

"You do realize the tea probably comes from some ten-gallon bag of tea syrup made in a sweat shop somewhere." Often in business, the customer was told only what they wanted to hear. No doubt, the catering staff did the same, and then laughed about the pretentious, politically correct picnickers. "I know. I just thought I'd get into the spirit of things. It will help me loosen up before I run into Ellie." He placed an apple chip in his mouth and chewed meditatively.

Picking up a chip from his own plate, he found the taste light, different, but somewhat intriguing. Rather like Nina, he almost laughed at the comparison. He doubted he'd encounter the woman. Pammy was probably as close as either one of them would get to an interested female. Daniel, as if channeling his thoughts, coughed.

"There she is," he whispered.

When Tony tried to turn to see who was there, he got a sturdy kick under the table.

"Don't look," he added with a smitten smile, "She's here,"

Nina would be with her, but Daniel forbade him to look. He turned, anyway, not seeing the women in question. "Where are they?"

"Ellie drifted off to the lake. I'm going after her." Daniel stood, wiping his mouth and hands, pushing his shoulders back as if going into battle.

"Do you want me to go with you?" Tony half-stood, ready to find the enigmatic Nina.

His friend pinned him with a glare, which needed no interpretation. "No, I don't want you to go. I can handle this myself."

Sinking back into his seat, Tony threw up his hands in mock surrender. Daniel strolled off just about the time the tea arrived. He'd drink the second glass too. If Daniel didn't come back promptly, then he'd start his search.

Chapter Eleven

THE SOUNDS OF her friend cheerfully singing about girls having fun while she got herself ready caused Nina to question her own attitude. The mirror reflected back the same face, she'd seen all her life, maybe a little older, but the expression confused her. Running a brush through her long, dark hair, she pondered her eyes. How were they different? One thing she did know, she lacked both the energy and anticipation Ellie carried in buckets.

The week from hell sucked out all her vitality, leaving her in such a lethargic funk she did well to crawl out of bed. Nina pulled her hair up into a high ponytail and secured it with a hair tie. She could fake perky with the hair. The idea raised her eyebrows, but it might be because she fastened the hairband too tight. Loosening it gave her a less arched appearance. If she wanted to be honest with herself—and she wasn't too sure she did—she wasn't feeling it. By the time the two of them walked to the lake, the community would be in holiday frenzy. Of course, with her neighborhood, it might be harder to gauge the mood upswing, but she could.

Because it was a holiday, many of the men would start drinking early. One of them might talk to her, which was a sign in itself. Robert Downton, who took such pride in tracing his bloodline back to England, would mention his ancestor was Queen Elizabeth's lover.

Then the man would strike a pose with his hands on his hips, his meager chest pushed out, and his right leg in front of his left as if ready to start skipping. Anyway, that's what happened at the Christmas festivities.

A gossipy woman from the gym, whose name started with a C or a K, Cathy, Colleen, or Krista, would confide in her that the holiday parties involved a certain amount of swinging. Krista felt the need to tell her since many of her formerly reticent neighbors would hit on her as new and different from their wives.

Seen in a different light, Robert's behavior could be his version of a come-on. Who knew how far he'd have gone to make his point? His cool blonde wife, Laribeth, gathered him up as if he was one of their children. As she left, her eyes had flicked toward Nina. Pursing her lips, she acted as if she had tasted something bad.

Nina had to concede she was different from Laribeth. Taller, rounder, darker, and less starch for sure. The Laribeths of the world managed to sail on untroubled waters as if they were tall ships while she chugged about resembling a determined towboat.

Her thought of unwanted advances from her neighbors almost flattened any desire to go to the party. She worked up enthusiasm for Ellie's sake. The magazine perfect decorating, the catered food, even the slow-moving residents moving across the green with the attitude and speed of stylishly garbed cows would impress Ellie. No doubt, she'd eat with gusto, drink too much, and shriek at the fireworks. Her unbridled enthusiasm would attract some married man whose wife had mentally left to become the perfect mother. For a minute, he'd trap Ellie in the dark for a passionate embrace, whispering words of his ability, until Nina extracted her friend from the cheater's embrace.

The upper class or pseudo-upper-class dynamics were twisted. The men slipped their marital collars for a few nights a year without too many consequences. No moving vans appeared a week after the holidays. When one did show, it was usually because the wife became too friendly with the golf pro, the tennis instructor, or the children's soccer coach. Suddenly they were willing to ditch their high earning husband for a tanned body, rock hard abs, and an accent. Talkative women explained all these intricacies to her at the Memorial Day picnic, which Nina forced herself to attend. Despite her efforts to attend events, she still felt disconnected from the whole neighborhood. With Ellie by her side, she was bound to have a good time.

As if hearing her thoughts, her friend slipped into the bathroom and pointed to her wrist. "Tick tock, tick tock."

"I know." She upended her makeup bag to locate the missing eyelash curler half hidden by the tubes of concealer and mascara. "Remember, we do not want to be the first ones there. It makes us look pathetic like we have no children to dress or husbands to nag to get ready."

Picking up the mascara, Ellie gave her eyelashes an extra coat. "True, true. I'm just so excited. I feel like something is going to happen. Don't you?"

Her friend's eyes glistened back from the mirror at her. Oh yeah, no doubt about it, she was wired. Nina's shoulders drooped even more if that were possible.

Poking a finger in her back, Ellie reminded her to stand up. "Ladies, our carriage is what makes us or breaks us." The phrase was a favorite of the modeling coach from the school both their mothers forced them to attend.

Without too much thought, she tucked her hips under and threw back her shoulders, which pushed her breasts out.

"Now that's what the men want to see."

Her words almost made her slump again. Who cared about the men? She didn't unless it was one man who appeared to have slipped away with the wrong impression that she hung out with wayward women. *Don't think about it,* she reminded herself as the same wayward friend tried on her lipstick.

"It's too dark for you." The words sounded abrupt and harsh to her ears.

"You're right." Ellie sunnily agreed and wiped it off with a tissue.

Goodness, she felt like she stomped on a baby chick, only the chick was unaware it had been stomped. Ellie wanted the same things she did, even if she went about it a different way. Apparently, Ellie's modus operandi, which rested mainly on latching on to anyone who showed the least bit of attention, was better than hers, which seesawed between fortune tellers who lied and men from online dating companies who also lied. At least, she hoped the fortune teller lied. If she lied, it meant Tony was not her soul mate. Biting her lips, she wondered if the thought liberated or depressed her.

"An old school beauty treatment," Ellie exclaimed and began to bite her lips.

Her actions made Nina's lips quirk up a little. She decided not to mention that wasn't her intention. She slipped her dress over her champagne lace bustier and tap pants.

Ellie remarked from her impromptu seat on the bathroom counter. "If I had underwear that looked that beautiful, I would just parade around in it. Plenty of women will be wearing less today with their short shorts and bikini tops."

Smoothing the dress in place, she checked herself in the mirror front on, sideways, and back, looking over her shoulder. For once, she had to admit she looked good.

Ellie whistled her approval before pushing on the counter. "The ponytail has to go. The dress screams sultry while the ponytail screams wholesome."

"I am wholesome." She wanted to argue the point, but wondered if too many men wanted to meet wholesome women outside of Bible Study.

Stretching to stand on her toes, her friend snagged the band from her hair but grunted with the effort. "This would be easier if you took off your heels."

Sliding one off, then another, she allowed her friend to finish her hairstyle change. The mirror revealed a hair snarl left behind she would need to pick out. Still, her friend was right. With her hair down, she needed dangling earrings too.

Thirty minutes later, they managed to walk out of the house. Ellie walked beside in her sunny yellow flowered dress, clutching a straw hat she insisted on bringing, but only cried. Her waterfall of natural blond hair would draw men like honey, especially paired with her cheerful personality. Nina hoped one or two wouldn't be married. If the dating gods were kind, one would be decent.

The patriotic bunting and food did not impress her. She'd seen twice the amount of grandiose pretensions at the Christmas display. The Fourth of July layout was a pale shadow of what the neighborhood association could do if they actually tried.

"Look at all the wonderful finger food and vegetarian selections." Ellie pressed her hand to her heart as if overcome.

She shook her head at her friend's antics. "You're not even a vegetarian."

"So?" Shrugging her shoulders nonchalantly, she considered the rest of her dining choices. "I appreciate diversity and presentation."

A server placed an ear of roasted bi-color corn on Nina's plate. Ellie pointed to her teeth, reminding her corn would stay in her teeth until she could floss. *Wonderful.* It was too late to give it back. A sharp knife would liberate the kernels from the cob.

Spotting a nearby empty table, they both sat. She was grateful to relax instead of tiptoeing on the balls of her feet, keeping her heels from sinking into the soil. She wondered how many rules she'd break by going barefoot. "For the December shindig, they brought in Santa and eight real life reindeers with a sleigh."

Ellie laughed. "I bet the children loved it. What about Rudolph?"

"Reindeers aren't that easy to get, especially around the holidays. They were grateful to get eight. I had no clue what surly creatures they were until Bunny Finley wrangled them for the Christmas party." She wrinkled her nose, remembering the crotchety Saint Nick and his overfed team.

"What happened?" Ellie asked as she peeped over her shoulder.

Nina didn't have to turn around to know a man or men stood in line. She chose to pretend her reindeer story riveted her friend. "I guess the reindeer were tired of being patted and petted. They were rather belligerent, stomping their hooves, waving their antler-laden heads, which was enough to put an eye out. One of the bratlings poked at a reindeer with a stick, and it had the nerve to snap at the offender. Oh my, the incident almost blew up in a court case. Another member declared it was cruelty to animals to have the creature out of their native tundra. Of course, she didn't realize they came from the Christmas Park Petting Zoo."

The waiter delivered the lemonades with a smile before rushing off to another table where the man loudly called "Garcon," and snapped his fingers.

Ellie nibbled on her gourmet burger while her mind naturally drifted elsewhere. An undefinable look crossed her face as she stood. "I need to check out something. I'll be right back."

Ellie's movement reminded her of the women in the old black and white horror movies enthralled by a vampire. Something outside, they called them, and they answered with sureness, often unaware they were even moving. While she did wonder where Ellie was going, she had no doubt she'd return shortly. The pressed sandwich with the avocado, provolone cheese, watercress, and Italian dressing drizzled over the ciabatta bread almost melted in her mouth. She savored it. How it brought back memories of Nona Caprice. How she missed her grandmother.

A few elderly couples moved through the assembly with upright posture and a head angle, which indicated knowledge of their superiority. They were as different from Nona Caprice as she could imagine. Her grandmother embraced everything with passion for cooking to loving. When she'd come to visit, she would grab Nina up in her arms and squeeze her as hard as she could, which was never too hard. Instead of frightening her, it reassured her of how much her Nona loved her. That's what was missing from this gathering.

No boisterous singing, often by the joy of being alive on such a beautiful afternoon, no men breaking into impromptu dancing with their wives when a familiar song played, no playful pats on the rear, no eating with gusto, no kids running around wild with their parents struggling to keep up. The best she could hope for was Robert Downton trapping her again with tales of his lascivious relative. Nope, come to think of it, her life and relationships were just as lackluster.

An image of Gavin plastering her to her car came to mind, but it was mere sex, not to be confused for passion. Half the time, she believed her dates often existed in a state of asexuality, but felt the need to convince her otherwise to assure future companionship. It usually worked out the other way, leaving her with no real regrets. She definitely had passion for her work. Right now, it happened to be her primary passion.

A downward glance revealed she had finished her plate except her corn. Odd, Ellie hadn't returned. It was best she checked to make sure one of the confused about their marital state males roaming the festivities hadn't waylaid her friend. Some men always appeared confused about their marital status, whom they owed allegiance to, and why they should keep their pants zipped. Ellie's gullibility drew the wrong men like a lodestone. She often thought a man who said he was going through a divorce meant he was in the middle of a divorce. His real meaning was he disliked the restrictions, marriage put on him and would like to be free to pick up attractive women.

Time to go rescue her bestie. She rose to her feet and turned slowly, trying to see her in the immediate area. All she got were a few masculine smirks, a couple winks, and a hand wave. Any response would have the waving bald man galloping in her direction. She set off in a direction directly opposite.

A few children ran among the trees screaming until a vigilant mother put a swift end to such behavior with a few terse words. Ducking into the more heavily wooded area, she surprised a teenage couple who eyed her anxiously, but did not let go of one another. That wasn't the case for Robert Downton and the woman he happened to be feeling up. He almost tossed the woman into the lake after Nina startled him with her unexpected entrance into the copse of trees.

At least she knew where Ellie wasn't. The next thing would be to circle the perimeter of the lake. Even though the actual size would be small by most estimates, hiking around it in a dress and heels on a hot July day failed to entice her. Ellie had possibly gone back to the house. Perhaps a wardrobe malfunction or something else sent her fleeing home. The solution appealed due to its closeness, and it would give her a pleasant air-conditioned break.

Ellie's car still sat in front of the garage. She hadn't left in a huff for an unknown reason, which meant she should be inside. Nina expected to hear music or something when she opened the family room door, not silence. A quick walk through proved no friend was in any room crying her heart out or bemoaning her fate. Kicking off her shoes, she sank into her overstuffed couch and propped her feet up on the coffee table. The ceiling fan created a breeze and shadows. Holding her hair up, she enjoyed the respite from the heat.

Letting her hair drop, she closed her eyes and managed to not think of anything, stilling the wheels in her head for a few precious seconds. This doing nothing was such a luxury. If Ellie found someone, there was no reason for her to go out again. What if she hadn't? What if her friend aerated the commons' lawn with her stilettos in her efforts to find her? Knowing Ellie, she would be convinced it was her responsibility to make Nina have a good time.

Two more seconds, no make it ten more seconds. That's all she asked. Ten seconds may have morphed into a few minutes or more, as she suddenly jerked awake. Goodness. If she didn't find Ellie soon, the woman might try to alert neighborhood security of her absence, giving Krista some new gossip. Forcing the heels back on her feet, she headed toward the lake. The lake appeared huge from this angle. Changing into a pair of flats would have been the smarter thing to do. A glance over her shoulder revealed the house to be equal distance to her as was the lake.

As she drew closer, she could see rowboats gliding across the water. She'd get into a boat. Slightly changing her path, she headed for the dock. Surely, she could row a boat. How hard can it be?

She held her shoes in her hand, as she gingerly stepped into the rowboat. The unsteady boat caused her to catch her breath more than a few times as she eased into a seating position on the bench seat. All right, she'd got into the boat without tipping it over. Pleased with her accomplishment, she rested back on her arms and looked at the rope securing the boat to the dock. Apparently, she'd need to lose the rope from the hook. Too bad, she hadn't considered unhooking the rope as she scampered onto the boat. Doing it now would mean more swaying and the possibility of ending up in the lake, not something she wanted.

Staying in her position, she considered how much she wanted the boat to move as opposed to how much she didn't want to end up on the water. A glance up at the dock showed a man walking toward her, just like her dream. She'd have to warn him to untie the boat first. Her breath caught in her throat. The urge to close her eyes tempted her. She wanted it to be Tony, but if it weren't, she'd just look foolish sitting in a rowboat with her eyes closed. Where was the fog from her dream?

Logically, she knew fog would have burned off by afternoon. Part of her urged her to leave now, go, before she could be disappointed or worse yet, screw things up. The man drew close enough for her to take in the details of his white shirt and light colored pants, the same as in her dream. Propelling herself out of the boat now would end up with her going head first into the water. In her effort to flee, she'd have to run past him.

Even though she vowed not to, she closed her eyes for just a second to gather her courage. Calmness settled over her, and she could Nona's voice. *"Live your life, Nina. Live with passion. Don't turn away from the good things. Have faith in me. This is a very good thing coming toward you."*

A laugh bubbled up out of her at the words. They were so Nona Caprice. Her eyelids flickered open, and he stood above her, gazing down at her with a playful grin. He squatted on one leg, placing one foot in the boat. It didn't rock as much with him or maybe he knew how to get into a boat. Shifting his weight, he eased the second foot in. Once in the boat, he flexed his knees, lowering his center of balance and picked the knot free. She would have to remember to do that.

The rope dropped back into the boat, allowing the boat to drift a bit. Up until then, he said nothing. He sat on the bench seat facing her and put his hands on the oars. His legs spread wide took up the maximum amount of space. Nina accommodated him by placing her feet into the open V. It seemed right.

"I figured this might be my best bet to talk to you since you always disappear on me." The oars dipped into the water propelling the boat into a glide across the water.

"It has merit. I'm glad you waited until you were in the boat to untie it." She ran her fingers through her hair grooming it, making sure no tangles had developed during her search, not like untying it first as in her dream.

He angled his body toward her, stopping the oars for a moment, but keeping his hands on them. "You dreamed about the boat too?"

His gaze held hers, sincere, mesmerizing. How did she miss those glorious eyes on her way out of the grocery store? Oh yeah, it was a reaction due to too much ginger. "I did, but there was a fog."

"Yes, the fog." He nodded and put his back into the rowing, moving the boat away from any neighboring crafts. He reached the middle of the lake and stopping. "I have tried to meet you, but all my efforts failed miserably."

"Hard to imagine you were trying to meet me." She touched his calf with her bare foot. This pleased her more than words could describe. This meeting was no random card trick of a fortune teller.

The oars rested in the locks, allowing the boat to drift a little with the current. Tony touched his neck. "Um, me climbing in the boat and taking off didn't scare you, did it? You didn't think here comes this crazy guy I don't know."

Using the side of her foot, she tapped his leg to get him to stop. "Please, no more. I knew you were supposed to get into the boat, just like I knew I had nothing to fear from you."

"Really?" His posture straightened as his right hand came up to touch his neck. "How is that?"

Fantastic. How could she explain this without sounding nutty? Biting her bottom lip, she wondered what she could say without mentioning soul mate or the fortune teller or the seven chances. The desire to count their meetings almost overwhelmed her senses to stay in the moment. Perhaps that's why his soft kiss on her lips surprised her.

He was already reassuming his seat as she stared in shock at the pleased man. How did he manage to slip the three feet to kiss her without rocking the boat? It had probably rolled a little, but she dismissed it since the water kept up a soft buffeting.

The boat moved as he dipped the oars back into the water. "I'm not sorry. I won't apologize for kissing you when you looked so indecisive. What was vexing you?"

"It's silly." She looked down at her hands, certain her color heightened. "I went to a fortune teller, although it was entirely unintentional."

Using only one oar, he began to turn the boat to make a thorough circuit of the lake. "Explain. Did she take you hostage?"

The description made her laugh a little. It made her sound more dramatic than she'd ever been. "No, nothing like that. I was heading to the spice store. It was such a beautiful day I decided to walk. I went past this curio shop crammed full of knick-knacks and figurines. A sign for Tarot Readings caught my eye. I couldn't even remember seeing the store there before. When I continued to the spice store, an elegant white-haired lady appeared between the buildings."

Tony nodded as he listened to her story. "So she wasn't a scary crone with bushy eyebrows and a mole on her nose?"

Thinking about the slender woman with her erect carriage, she shook her head. "Good Heavens, Helen would be appalled at such a description. She would fit in very well here." She gestured to the shore where couples strolled arm in arm. A few carried children or pushed them in high-wheeled carriages, which would be more appropriate hitched behind a trotting horse. Helen would consider her above the affluent residents, and she'd be right.

He toed off his shoes, and then looked up suddenly. "Sorry, I didn't ask if it was all right if I removed my shoes."

Nina angled her head and looked up through her lashes. "We're not in the Victorian times. Besides, you can take off your shoes. After all, I've seen you in my dreams and the crystal ball."

"Crystal ball, hmm, I don't think I've been in anyone's crystal ball before." His bare foot brushed hers.

At first, she thought it was an accidental touch until he slowly swept over her foot. That was no accident. Her toes curled, and there was no way to hide it. Did he notice? His contented expression announced he probably did. The attraction between them almost glowed. Did she want to ruin it by talking about what she saw in the small globe? Her logical side advised her to change the direction of the conversation. Still, something deeper, perhaps even older, pushed the words out of her mouth before she had a chance to draw them back.

"I saw you in the crystal ball. The first image was my first day in school. You stood on the steps with a superhero backpack. You looked at me as if you recognized me." He didn't appear too weirded out by the information.

"Do you remember which superhero it was?" His eyes flickered upward as he tried to remember.

"Hey, I'm a female. Superheroes were not a part of my life. I remember you had on a red shirt."

A pair of screeching children ran beside the lake, waving sparklers followed by an indulgent older man. Tony nodded to the pair. "It looks like they're having fun."

"Now they are, but just wait. Mother will come and put a stop to it." A woman in matching capris and top rushed down the bank. She removed the nearly spent sparklers from the children's hands and tossed them into the lake. The two boys walked back toward the cupola, their heads down and feet dragging. The woman had a few sharp words to say to the man who appeared almost as defeated as the children.

Tony watched the entire scene and shook his head. "The children were only having fun. Why did she scold them?"

"Good question." Her shoulders went up in a search me gesture. "I've lived here almost a year, and I still don't understand the social contract. There's a homeowner's contract that specifies not leaving cars in the driveway overnight, garbage cans cannot linger outside past eight pm on garbage day, and there's this other unwritten social contract I didn't receive, but most people seem to know."

He leaned forward slightly and inhaled. "Did I mention you smell wonderful? I'm also aware of your effort to change the conversation away from the crystal ball. This is very unfair of you." He winked at her.

Her heart turned over. God, she was acting like such a girl. His wink had twice the effect it had on her at the concert. She fought hard not to sigh and bring her hands to her heart like a cartoon heroine. "You saw through my weak efforts?'

"I did. I was older than you were which explains the red shirt. Second graders wore red shirts at Oberon. Why can I not remember any Ninas at Oberon? It was a small school."

Ah, he would have to turn over that stone. Sighing deeply, she said, "I changed my name from Angioletta to Nina when I was in fifth grade. You were probably in sixth by then."

"Ah, I remember you now. It all makes sense." His broad grin announced his amusement. "Angioletta, which means little angel, from what I heard, didn't live up to her name. The tales of your misdeeds were rampant from telling all the struggling readers how the storybooks ended to giving a few boys well deserved kicks in the family jewels on the playground."

"Surely, I wasn't that bad." If she ever had to watch a video based on her life to gain entrance through the pearly gates, she had a feeling her early years might be a detriment. "I was just a trifle high-spirited."

"Yes, that's what she calls it." He looked down at their feet, placed the side of his foot on her ankle and rubbed it up and down her exposed calf. "No wonder you don't understand these mothers. They won't even allow their children to have sparklers on the only holiday you're supposed to play with fire. Tell me more about what you saw in the ball."

She hesitated, wondering if the scenes would paint her in an unflattering light, since the innocent first day of school turned out to be releasing the devil on the unsuspecting Oberon Elementary School. His foot caressed her leg, raising her temperature, making her want to pull him into her arms. So far, she kept her movements very small, not wanting to tip the boat. A dunk in the middle of the lake would definitely quench their ardor. Nor did her dress lend itself to swimming.

"The second image was my first day at college, and I was unload-ing my car."

Touching her foot, he commented, "I know this one. This Italian beauty was staggering underneath this tall box. My plan was to help her and earn her gratitude. I screwed it up. She told me her room number. What a fool I was. My goal was to impress you with how strong and capable I was. Of course, I arrived at your room way before you did. I waited, but since it was a girl's dorm some of the mothers were giving me the stare down, so I left."

Feeling daring, she leaned forward and tapped his knee playfully. "I wish you would have come back around. I wanted to make you a cake or at least an oversized cookie. This handsome upperclassman shows up and helps me, then disappears. The reason it took me so long to make it to my room is your non-helpful frat brothers were hitting on me and not carrying a blessed thing. If you are wondering, I didn't go out with any of them, but I would have gone out with you."

He pulled hard on one oar, spinning the boat.

"What are you doing?" She whooped with delight at his show of spontaneity. He was obviously not a neighborhood resident. He stopped rowing and allowing the boat to slow to a rock.

"It was as close as I could get to spinning in a circle, yelling woo-hoo to the fact you wanted to go out with my scrawny sophomore self."

"Of course, I did. It wasn't only because you were handsome, which I had to have been blind not to have noticed. Your actions said more. Nona Caprice told me a man's actions spoke more loudly than his words. When you showed up for the interview at McMillian and Sons, I had to tell you the job was no longer available due to a case of rampant nepotism. You were kind to me and thanked me while the chick snorted at me and slammed out of the building." A sense of aggravation filled her at the injustice at placing incompetent relatives in salaried positions. Later, she learned it was an unfortunate practice in businesses.

"Ah, yes, I remember it well." His eyes lit up as if the memory pleased him. "This gorgeous woman whose face I only saw briefly comes out and mumbles something about the job no longer being available, which wasn't a big deal since I had several more interviews. All I wanted was for her to look at me, which she did only briefly when we shook hands. You even smiled briefly. I lived on the memory of your smile and hope for a good two weeks. I even went back to inquire if you were still there." He stared down at his hands.

"Really, you went back for me?" The thought made her beam. "The receptionist didn't give you any information, did she?" Did she have anyone who had ever returned to look for her? Nona Caprice knew the hearts of men or at least this man.

"Legally she was not allowed to even able to say your name, which made me think you went out in a blaze of glory." He winked at her again, which made her feel they had some sort of camaraderie going.

Nina swallowed hard. "You could say that. Thank goodness, I already had my next job. My hotheaded grade school ways were still with me a little then. I was so upset after making you wait, only to tell everyone to go home because the bumbling nephew would take the job. I wished them the joy of their nephew and walked out. I never could use them for a reference. It was my last show of spite in the work world."

Tony leaned forward to catch her hands. He brought each hand to his lips and kissed the backs. Releasing her, he said, "No woman has ever cared enough about me to trash her own reference."

The man had to be dating some ice-cold females if they didn't adore this man or sell their soul for him. She was going overboard, but she felt as if she knew him on a much deeper level than she could explain. Taking a chance, she mentally girded herself. "Do you want to know what else the fortune teller told me?"

Tony wiggled his eyebrows up and down. "I think I am going to like this."

Holding a finger to her lips, she waited until he was silent. "This is very serious. After my first visit, I went back to see her, but I couldn't find her or her shop, and the local police said many people claim to have met her and gone into her shop, and then couldn't find her or it afterward."

Keeping his lips shut, he pointed to her, then cupped his ear, then pointed to himself. She understood. Nina just wasn't sure if she wanted to tell him all about it. It might end up scaring or make her sound needy or stupid, but she'd come this far. She slid one hand over another until she was wringing her hands. His hands landed on hers, stopping the action.

"Where's my little angel? The one who ruined the semester for reading teachers and told her boss what he could do with himself. Channel that fearless female. Remember, nothing you say will chase me away if you are worried. It took me years to get into the boat." One hand reached up to stroke her cheek.

"Okay, here's the rest." She turned one hand over to grip his. "Helen told me you were my soul mate and not everyone has one. In this life, I had seven chances to connect with you. I had met you three times already. I only had four more changes, and if I didn't connect, I was done for this lifetime."

Chapter Twelve

SOUL MATE. THOSE were his mother's words. Someday, she hoped he would find his soul mate, and when he did, he'd know. The same romantic foolishness that filled the romance novels, his mother devoured. Up to that moment, he would have labeled it nonsense, but none of the previous women he'd encountered had ever caused this feeling. His hand covered his heart. It felt as if it were trying to jump out of his chest and into the floor of the boat like a landed trout.

The beautiful woman regarded him intently. Her fingers entwined with his tugged slightly, indicating a desire to pull free. Instead of letting go, he tightened his grasp slightly. Her teeth worrying her bottom lip showed signs of being nervous. Why would she be so anxious?

A glance at the lake revealed the water as calm as before, causing their small craft to gently bob in the water. No motorized boats tore across the water, creating wakes and throwing water. A few rowboats similar to theirs dotted the surface. It couldn't be him, could it? If so, why would she be suddenly agitated? Has she been that way all along? The high-handed way he untied and jumped into the boat came to mind. "Nina, are you afraid of me?"

Her eyes met his. "No, Antonius. Why would I be afraid of you?"

Her gaze held his, her chin firm, but he had the feeling she was a good poker player. He looked into the eyes of a bluffer, usually a successful one. "It's Tony now."

"I know," she said softly and pulled her hand from his to lace her fingers together in her lap.

Deciding if that was a good sign or not was difficult. The two of them couldn't sit in the boat and drift across the lake, either. Should he tell her he changed his last name to Dante? Maybe, but right now, he wanted to win her over, bond her to him. Talking about his father's misdeeds would not impress her. "Wait, you did call me Tony earlier. How did you know? Did Ellie tell you?"

"No." Her glance slipped away from him and looked toward the shore.

Two children edged closer to the shore, throwing stones into the water. An efficient mother would show up on the scene and haul the rule breakers away. Strange there would even be rocks around to toss, which meant it was probably landscaping stone.

Nina started speaking, still looking away from him. "When I thought of you after I saw you at the grocery store and concert, Antonius no longer fit. Tony did."

She pivoted on the seat from staring at the rock-throwing children to look at him. "I know it sounds ridiculous, right up there with finding a soul mate." A laugh, more of a snort, sounded. The horrified look on her face told him it hadn't sounded the way she planned. There was a good chance she might decide to jump overboard and swim to shore. Bending at the hips, he managed to capture her hands. Pulling them apart, he laced his fingers with hers, enjoying the feel of her slender, elegant fingers entwined with his. Holding up their hands, the image reminded him of his grandparents.

"My grandparents always held hands like this. Some of my

grandmother's friends would tuck their hands into the curve of their husband's bent arm, treating him like a wedding usher. Nona Maria would say hers was not a formal relationship, but a love match. Lovers who wove their fingers together could not be broken apart."

Nina's eyes developed a sheen, suspiciously like tears. "You had an Italian Grandmother too? I guess I should expect it with a name like Antonius."

The desire to make her smile to counteract the tears in her eyes pressed on him with as much urgency as he'd ever felt before. "What a name for a little boy. It's an ancient Roman name. Perhaps the original owner did something noteworthy, such as developing indoor plumbing."

Her smile appeared, small and uncertain, but it showed just the same, similar to the dawn after spring storm, very much welcomed.

"The Romans did have an aqueduct system carrying water to and from their households. Maybe, an Antonius designed it all." Her smile grew a little wider, but a tear still trickled down her cheek.

Letting go of one hand, he used his index finger to brush it away.

"Oh my goodness, you must think me foolish, tearing up over Roman names, and aqueducts, and such."

Scooting forward, he angled his body to balance his weight on his wide spread knees and kissed her still moving lips. Her squeeze of their connected hands assured him of her reception. Her lips moved under his, kissing him back. Now he understood. His free hand went to her thick hair, working his fingers through her tresses. Nina tantalized all his senses from her thick locks where he buried his fingers to her soft lips. A spicy rose aroma wrapped around him, he would always associate with her and this moment. Her lips managed to be soft, firm, and passionate all at the same time.

A whistle from the shoreline broke through the enchantment, along with a single pair of hands clapping. Confused, he pulled away, or more truthfully, Nina did. No one in the community would be so crass to comment on a kissing couple, but the clapping would not stop. He looked to the shore to see Daniel waving at them, a petite blonde beside him.

Nina fussed with her hair, finger-combing it forward to hide her flushed cheeks. He understood her embarrassment. Reclaiming her hand, he interwove their fingers again. "Look at me."

She raised hesitant eyes to his.

"We did nothing wrong. You have nothing to be embarrassed about. We both are single, available people who happen to be attracted to one another. We shared a kiss in a boat. A very romantic gesture, which probably made most of those ice queens on shore melt with envy. If there is some ridiculous rule about not showing public affection, then you need to move elsewhere." He stopped abruptly, afraid it sounded too much like a lecture or advice, which it was.

Glancing at their hands, then up to his face, a mischievous twinkle entered her eyes. "Why might I need to think about moving?"

Ah yes, the real Nina was back. The one who would kick a man in the nut sack if needed. The man at the concert got off easy. His spontaneous decision to tell her his plans might be dangerous since he was not sure how she'd react. The good news was the lake was man-made and appeared to be relatively shallow, which meant he could probably walk to shore if needed. "There will plenty of affection between us. I plan on holding your hand, kissing you, and even giving you a slap on the ass, in public, despite your neighbors giving me the evil eye."

Nina rounded her mouth in fake surprise. Her laughing eyes gave her away. "What if I don't like this?"

"I must not be doing it right then. I'll have to try harder, channeling all the great lovers throughout history. I am not letting go of you because you *are* my soul mate. Apparently, this is my last chance.

I'd be a fool to lose you yet again."

The tears he'd wiped away earlier re-appeared in her eyes. Her voice trembled as she asked, "Am I your soul mate?"

He reached into his pocket for the small box. "On some level, I must have known you'd be here. My mother gave this to me. It came from my great grandmother. My great grandfather created it for her."

Thumbing open the box, he presented the glass medallion. It featured a rose growing out of where two hearts touched. Nina carefully withdrew the pendant and held it up to the light. Sunlight backlit the glass, making it glow.

"It's beautiful. I've never seen anything like it."

The necklace dangled from her fingers, throwing splashes of color onto her face. He could see the image of the hearts and flower on her cheek, making an almost translucent tattoo. "My great grandfather was a glassblower and considered quite talented in the field. My great grandmother was his inspiration. He even devised a shade of blue to match her eyes."

"What a romantic story." Nina clasped her hands together and grinned.

He took the necklace from her unresisting fingers and opened the clasp. Nina, anticipating his intentions, held her hair and twisted in the seat to present her back to him. Reaching around her, he encircled her neck with the chain before fastening it. With his mouth to her ear, he finished the tale.

"My great grandfather was not the man picked for my great grandmother. She came from a noble family long on bloodline and pride while great granddad was a tradesman."

Nina interrupted the tale. "An artist, not a tradesman."

Dropping a kiss on her neck, he murmured, "That's not how they saw it."

Nina leaned back into his arms, which unfortunately caused the boat to list a little, startling her to sit back up. Due to it being a flat-bottomed boat it didn't roll, but it destroyed the moment. Resuming her seat, she urged him to continue. "What happened then?"

No help for it, he might as well row for shore where Daniel waved while the blonde clapped her hands as if applauding a dramatic performance. No doubt, Nina would like to avoid being the star of the holiday festivities. Putting his hands on the oars, he began to glide backwards. Eventually, he'd have to turn the boat around to dock it.

"Great Granddad Vincenzo did what all Italian men would do at the time to assure a woman remained his." He winked, knowing where her mind might go.

Her expression intent, she said, "He declared his love."

"No." He checked over his shoulder to find the dock. "They both had declared their love for one another, and it made no impression on her parents who had an older, wealthy man picked out for her."

Her brow beetled up as she concentrated. When he realized he was grinning like a fool, thinking how cute her furrowed forehead looked, he knew he was lost, just like Great Granddad.

"They ran off to America together," she announced with a triumphant expression.

He nodded his head, recognizing the answer. "It would have been a good choice, but no, that wasn't it."

Her frustration started to show by the mulish line of her lips. "What is it? They couldn't have killed themselves like Romeo and Juliet because there would be no you." She tempered her exasperation with a sideways glance. "I am glad there is a you."

Turning the boat slightly with one oar, he had the dock in view. Apparently, Daniel and friend had recognized their destination and stood on the dock. He'd needed to wind up the story quickly, but her last remark caught, leaving his heart in her hands. "I am very glad I am here too. My great-grandparents worked hard to make sure I existed, although not their thought at the time. They went to her father's choice for suitor and explained that she was expecting. Not exactly, what a man wanted to hear, especially when he knew it wasn't his. Great grandma willingly destroyed her reputation to marry the man she loved. Ironically, grandpa did not show up for another eighteen months, which begs the question did they lie."

"They did lie. So you implied all Italian men sleep with the women they love, but it appears they waited until after the wedding." Her eyebrows lifted in question.

"Think what you want. They aren't here to tell us. What I do know is my great grandmother treasured the necklace you are wearing. She gave it to her son with the instructions to give it to his soul mate, which he did. My mother's mother gave it to her. She handed it to me with instructions to save it for my soul mate. She told me I would know. I just about forgot about it until I was getting ready to leave this morning. Something made me go back and get it."

Nina held up the glass and rubbed it against her cheek. "Magic, that's what it was. I can feel it embedded in the glass. Years of loving soaked into the necklace. I feel honored to wear it. Thank you."

Angling his head toward the dock, he said, "Know any of those people?"

Ellie's face glowed and she shivered with excitement. "There's Ellie with that guy from the restaurant. Is he your friend?"

"Guilty as charged. That would be Daniel who insisted on dragging me to this event."

He watched the corners of her lips turn down. Did he say something wrong? It made him sound like he didn't want to be there. "I didn't know I would meet you."

"Who invited you? There aren't too many single women in the community. Unless a married woman was bold enough to offer an invitation."

The way her eyes narrowed didn't bode well for the other single women in the neighborhood. The moment of jealousy pleased him, but she needed to know the truth before they stepped ashore.

"Ellie invited Daniel, even to the point of giving up your security code." Jealousy disappeared only to give away to a mild confusion as she regarded her smiling friend on the dock. "I'm willing to bet she didn't mention it."

"Ok, I will admit Ellie was drunk last Sunday. A couple of times she wanted to tell me something, and I cut her off. I figured she would only apologize some more. She was trying to tell me or she forgot. In the end, it doesn't matter since we finally met."

Tony threw the rope to Daniel helped her up, giving her a little boost on the rear, which earned him a knowing look. She didn't need help. It made him laugh.

Ellie bounced from foot to foot until her friend's feet touched wood, catching her hands and exclaiming over the coincidence of meeting her old middle school crush.

Nina eyes met Tony's before saying. "It must have been fate. How else would he know you'd be here?"

Daniel appeared to be choking, and Nina gave him two hard whacks on the back.

It was the end of their private time, but it wasn't the end of the night. Joining her on the dock, their hands naturally drifted to one another. They walked hand in hand, while Daniel and Ellie extolled them with all they'd done.

The night began to settle, causing people to search out the best seats for the show. Most clumped around the rental circular tables and hard plastic chairs. Nina sighed, trying to settle into the chair. "Well, this is certainly uncomfortable. What I wouldn't give for a blanket."

Stripping the patriotic tablecloth off the table, Tony spread it on the ground. Bowing low, he gestured to the cloth. "Your impromptu blanket awaits, my lady."

They both settled on the ground. Daniel made a move to join him, but an abrupt move of Tony's head made his point. Let the man find his own blanket. The fireworks shot into the sky, showering them with light and sound. Nina settled back against his chest. The fireworks were a celebration, not only the nation's birthday, but also of two soul mates finding each other. How rare was that?

The night ended with a prolonged goodbye in the shadows of the trees surrounding Daniel's car. He offered to walk Nina home, but she assured him she had Ellie. They kissed one last time, after talking about a busy week and meeting again.

Halfway home, he realized he never got her number. He placed his heart in her hands, his soul at her feet, wrapped his remaining heirloom around her neck, and not once did he offer his number. She didn't offer hers, either. Did he read her wrong?

"Daniel, do you think Nina likes me? I'm not misreading any-thing, am I?" The doubt in his voice frightened him. Had he done it again, gone after a female who wasn't right for him?

"Ellie and I were surprised the brass band didn't switch to love songs while the two of you were kissing in the boat. A few of the Botox crowd smiled so hard their jawbones may have snapped." He chortled at his own perceived wit.

Tony wasn't sure. The only way he could be was to talk to Nina tomorrow. Maybe Daniel could get her number from Ellie.

Chapter Thirteen

NINA ALLOWED HER friend to ramble on and on about the wonders of Daniel. It was good to hear her friend so pleased. Maybe this man would treat her well. Heavens knew she deserved it. Her thoughts replayed the day with Tony. He was exactly what she needed, a straight-talking male with a passionate, romantic soul.

The fact he didn't stay the night disappointed her a little, but she didn't really want to be a booty call. It would have been awkward. Would she have kicked Ellie out of her house? There was no easy way to make it happen. If her destiny were for more to come, it would occur. She had no doubts, but felt fate might need a little nudge.

Her body recognized him as her other half. When they were watching the fireworks, his body cradled hers perfectly. There seemed to be an element of having known each other previously. As wonderful as the day had been, her yawn reflected her tiredness.

"Am I boring you?" Ellie teased, walking backward, trying to see Nina's face in the tastefully muted streetlights, which gave out about as much light as a candle in a cavern.

She attempted to swat Ellie, who danced out of her reach. What she wouldn't give to have as much energy. "It has been a long week."

They walked the few blocks to her house, nodding at families they met on the way. Entering through the back door, Nina confessed, "That is as much interaction I've had with my neighbors since the Christmas party."

Ellie laughed along with her at the absurdity of the statement. A trio of notes kept repeating in the background, making Nina wonder why they sounded familiar.

Ellie's head swung side to side. "I hear my phone, but forgot where I put it." The two of them scoured countertops, moved pillows, even checked bathrooms. Ellie located it near the microwave. "Found it."

By then, it had stopped chirping. Her friend scrolled through the messages. "There are almost a dozen here from my neighbor Kelley. I asked her to take care of Mr. Bigg."

Nina turned away so her friend didn't detect any distaste on her face. She wasn't a cat lover to begin, and Mr. Biggs rubbed her the wrong way all the time. The cat reminded Nina of all of Ellie's old boyfriends, spoiled, demanding, and not the least bit grateful. He probably had a cat food meltdown without Ellie to cater to his demanding self. Kelley probably didn't sing to him and stroke him while he ate.

She could hear the conversation between Ellie and Kelley. It started out with "No, no, what do you mean? Absolutely not... No, I am on my way."

Ellie's bubbly mood sprang a major puncture indicated by her trembling lips. "Justin's been at my house."

"Okay, then it was good you were over here. No reason for you to want to see that loser." Nina secretly feared he might be able to talk his way around Ellie. His kind always did. Still, she didn't understand why she was so upset about it.

Her friend gulped and shook her head. "I don't want him back unless he's dead," she finished with a snarl.

Her soft and fluffy bunny friend had turned into a wolverine in the last two seconds. "What did he do?"

Opening her mouth wide, she made a few gasping sounds trying to talk, but swallowed tears instead. Wrapping an arm around her, Nina guided her to the couch and eased her down. "Tell me."

Inhaling, Ellie firmed her jaw and choked back a sob. "Well, we know the bastard still has my key. Kelley said he let himself in. Since she lives in the duplex next to me, she heard someone tossing things around through the shared wall. Figured it was a robbery and called the police. She stood outside on the front walk and saw Justin leave. She didn't go in until the police came. When they walked in, she saw Mr. Biggs with a chef's knife through his body."

Nina hugged her friend tightly. True, she may not have liked Mr. Grumpy Bigg, as she called him, but no one had a right to do that. "Are the police still there?"

"No, they couldn't wait all night for me. I need to talk to them and press charges against Justin. I also need to go home and take care of Mr. Bigg." She covered her face as she began to cry in huge, noisy gulping sobs.

Rocking her, she comforted her friend. "Sweetie, it isn't good to go now. It's too late, and you're tired."

Breaking out of her embrace, Ellie looked at her in shock. "What type of feline companion would I be if I left Mr. Biggs there with a knife through his body? He would look like a phone message."

Phone message. Knife through body. Okay, she got it, referring to pink phone messages on spikes. Ellie watched a lot more vintage movies than she did. "I'm going with you."

"You're tired," Ellie pointed out, stood up, and gathered up her things. She put her hand on her small overnight bag, but Nina wrestled it from her.

"Think. Justin has the key. You are not safe there. I'm not letting you stay. I wish I had a gun, but I do have mace. Let's go take care of

Mr. Bigg, and then we are coming back here to sleep. Obviously, you will need your lock changed." She placed the suitcase down with a thump.

Ellie's already pale face blanched as she whispered the words, "He could come back?"

Bending her knees to look into her eyes, she said, "Yes, he could. He has a key. You are not safe there. You might want to get some more clothes until we work something out." She hated the pain her friend had to go through to realize what a creep Justin was. It was a form of shock therapy to wean her off the bad boy types.

Ellie's delicate hands scrunched into tiny fists. "I hope he does come back. I'll get revenge for Mr. Bigg."

"Let's hope he doesn't come back, or you might end up dead." Of course, she wondered if they both could end up dead. Going over there wasn't her brightest idea, but she knew she couldn't dissuade Ellie. The best she could do to help was to grab her cat and get out there. She had no clue what they would do with him. Couldn't bury him on her property. They probably had closed circuit cameras on all the light posts and trees. The city laws forbade internment of household pets because it affected the ground water. These same rules, however, didn't prevent birds from falling out of trees or animals drowning in streams.

Ellie held a tissue box to her chest. She alternated between crying, blowing her nose, and cursing Justin. "I should have been there to protect Mr. Bigg."

Thank God, she wasn't. Nina picked up the keys to her car. No way could Ellie drive. She'd probably end up running off the road in her present state. Passing through the garage, she grabbed some weighty garbage bags.

Ellie eyed the bags as she threw them in the backseat. "What are those for?"

Did she really have to ask? Did she not know? There was no way she was going to mention it. Instead, she gave her friend a long look, which caused her to erupt into a spate of crying. The very thing she was trying to avoid. On the way over, she played with the radio searching for something cheery and upbeat. A few stations were having tributes to all who died in war to keep us free. Nina wasn't sure how it related to an overweight, cantankerous feline, but it made Ellie cry even harder. Then there were the melancholy stations, which tempted her to bawl with their sad songs of loss and unrequited love. The short trip had to have been the closest thing to purgatory she ever hoped to experience.

Kelley stood outside the duplex waiting for them. A brave move on her part, knowing Justin was free to roam and liable to return. They walked into the duplex with one woman on either side of the crying Ellie. A sour chemical smell slipped under the door and circled their ankles, not fetid odor she expected. She'd had a few pets kick the bucket and walked past a decaying bird before. None of them smelt like that.

Looking over Ellie's head, she mouthed the words, "What is that smell?"

"Don't know. Police took samples. It's why I brought rubber gloves." She flourished a couple pairs of gloves, clutched in her hand. "As I told her on the phone, the bastard wrecked the place. I am only thankful she was with you. He probably thought she'd be at home feeling sorry for herself. Don't know what his plans were. Seeing her car gone did not make please him. I called the police since I was too scared to go over on my own."

"Good thing you did." Nina was grateful for a rational thinking neighbor.

Ellie put her hand on the doorknob and twisted, but found it locked. She looked up with a confused look on her face.

Kelley took a key from her pocket and opened the door. She stood in the doorway, blocking their view, but not the smell, which increased in strength, enough to make the three of them cough and their eyes water. Leaning against the door jam, she managed to gasp out. "Do you really want to do this?"

Ellie pushed her out of the way. "I have to take care of Mr... my God, what happened?"

Furniture lay on its side. Some were even upside-down as if a giant had thrown it in a capricious moment. Books, paper, and broken glass littered the floor, covered with a smoking liquid, which ate its way through the materials.

Nina warned, "Don't touch it. I am not sure what it is, but if it is eating through your couch, it will definitely do a number on your fingers." She glanced back at the rubber gloves Kelley still held. "Rubber probably won't save us, either."

Ellie turned slowly in a circle, taking in the wanton destruction. "What am I going to do?"

She acted as if she'd lost her last friend. Well, she did lose the last male who was always there for her even if he did have claws and a litter box. She doubted the overweight Himalayan would have willingly left the house. "Tomorrow, we'll call the claims adjuster. We will get a copy of the police report. Get your lock changed and call a crime scene cleanup unit."

"A CSI group like on television," Kelley added.

Nina managed a tired, half smile for the neighbor. "Not exactly, those people investigate the crime. We know who did it. We need someone to neutralize whatever is soaking into everything. The police might be able to suggest someone."

A shriek came from the kitchen indicating Ellie's location. "Mr. Bigg!"

One look at the stiff feline indicated there would be no singing to him at meal times. Ellie reached for the knife despite the shouted warnings not to. Nothing happened. Apparently, the cat had bled out all over the cabinets. Ellie held the knife by her side crooning to the dead cat. If Justin showed enough stupidity to return then, he'd be a dead man for sure.

Nina opened the freezer expecting food. A few ice cube trays, a couple of diet entrees were the entire contents. She dumped both items on the counter, then donned a pair of rubber gloves, courtesy of Kelley, picked up Mr. Bigg, and put him in the freezer.

"What are you doing?" Ellie dropped the knife and looked at the freezer.

Nina stepped over the knife and wrapped an arm around the grieving woman's shoulders. "I know you will want to have a funeral for Mr. Bigg. The freezer is the best way to preserve his body until we can get him to the pet cemetery. Let's go. You've done all you could. Tomorrow we'll make calls and make sure Justin pays."

The drive home was a battle to stay awake. She alternated blasting air conditioning with annoying talk radio, adding her own comments, especially when people called up with stupid, stupid questions. The current caller went out with someone she met online who confessed he was in an open marriage and his wife was fine with it. She wanted to know if she should keep seeing him.

"Run, fool, run."

Ellie muttered in her sleep, thinking her spoken comments were part of her dream. Nina decided to table her remarks to not wake her sleeping friend. The rest of the ride home was reasonably silent. She turned off the radio, not trusting herself to withhold her opinion of people who were ignorant enough to call a talk radio show to have their lives dissected in front of whoever listened late at night.

Due to the lack of cars on the road, Nina judged it to be past midnight. Turning into her neighborhood, she was surprised to see a guard at the gate. She punched in her code and asked, "What's up?"

"Complaints of strangers at the celebration and a show of raucous high spirits. A couple was even making out in public, in a rowboat, no less." The guard repeated the complaints in a sarcastic tone.

"Oh really." The attitude underlined the fact this neighborhood was not the place for her. "It must have happened after I left. I didn't see any of it."

The homeowners' association rule about not parking in the driveway proved beneficial for once. No one would witness her helping Ellie into the house. If spotted, they would assume she was drunk, not sleepy. Who had the time to report all these offenses? All she knew was she was tired of the pettiness. This wasn't the place for her. Ellie mentioned it once. Tony echoed her sentiments when the children couldn't even run around with sparklers. First, she'd get Ellie fixed up, then she'd put her house on the market. No clue where she'd move to, but any place should be better than this. There were some benefits to the neighborhood, with the front gate being one, though it wouldn't have helped Ellie. She would have given Justin her gate code, and he would have still done the evil thing no matter where she lived. Gates, guards, and fences didn't always protect you. The first protective measure was not to date the deadbeat creep to begin with.

THE WEEKEND DISAPPEARED under the pressures of taking care of Ellie. She spent too much time in the police annex, from pressing charges to getting the names of a clean-up crew. Mr. Biggs kept a frosty wait until the office of *Nap in Peace* opened on Monday. Ellie ended up buying clothes for work since her home wouldn't be available for use until Wednesday.

The claims adjustor gave them the most problem, suggesting Ellie wanted to remodel her house and savaged it on her own. While this torqued up Nina's anger level, her friend marched to the kitchen and game back with the frozen bloody feline. Frozen, blood matted hair was not a good look for Mr. Bigg.

"Did I kill my cat too for new furniture?" She shrieked the words, causing the man to make a few notations on his clipboard.

He handed the paper to Nina, while cutting his eyes at Ellie who was petting the dead cat. "Ok, your claim is good. Here, I'll write you a check for the full amount." While he wrote the check on the upturned bookshelf, his gaze kept going back to Ellie, who had gone to singing to her cat. It was obvious the man was desperate to leave. Nina was worried too.

He darted out of the door the same time Ellie returned the cat to the freezer and calmly asked, "Did we get the full amount?"

"We did." She high-fived her friend. Even though she was faking a little wacko to influence the reluctant agent, Nina was almost convinced it wasn't all an act. Who knew it would take so long to get to the clean-up stage? They still had the part where Ellie would have to select new furnishings to replace her damaged ones.

Her friend pushed something across the floor with her shod foot. There was enough left of the broken figurine to realize it used to be a pig. One of the many pigs Nina bought over the years to add to Ellie's pig collection.

Ellie's voice was flat and emotionless. "He destroyed everything."

The lack of anger surprised Nina. She knew she'd still be running on a high-octane fury by this time if it happened to her. A little anger and a thirst for revenge would make her feel better.

Still staring down at the broken pig, more to herself, Ellie said. "You warned me against Justin, told me he was no good, and was taking advantage of me. I thought you were jealous because I had a regular guy."

No use in second-guessing the situation. "I didn't like Justin because he never took you anywhere. That in itself was suspicious. You are a beautiful, charming female men should want to show off."

Her friend preened under her words, lifted up her head, and smiled faintly. Turning away from her contemplation of the broken pig, Ellie walked into the kitchen to wash her hands. Her voice echoed in the hard surfaced kitchen, distorting it a little. "I haven't forgotten you are taking me to the Candy Kitchen to drown my sorrows in chocolate."

This sounded more like the woman she knew. "Hurry, I think whatever chemical he used is searing my lungs." A series of coughs bent her over, emphasizing her point.

Ellie walked out of the kitchen, wiping her hands on her clothes. "I'm coming. I was thinking I could start a different collection since the pigs are gone."

The rest of the day consisted of speculating on if dragons were better than unicorns. At one time, Ellie considered getting figurines similar to Mr. Bigg, but Nina scotched the idea. Sure, she was sorry the cat was dead, but she drew the line at a shrine to him, which would only serve to keep Ellie in a semi-grieving mode.

Their evening consisted of Thai food, facial masks, and plans for a romantic comedy marathon. During the first movie, Ellie's phone rang. She could tell the way her friend's voice went up and changed to flirtatious banter it was a man. Justin was already in jail, but even if he wasn't, there was no way he could talk his way around Ellie. Killing a person's pet tended to turn them against you. Ellie gave her a small wave as she walked away with the phone to her ear to the guest bedroom.

Nina's finger rested on the remote, wondering if she should stop the movie. They were at the part where the romantic partners discover they are business rivals. Okay, she'd seen the movie before, but it was a good one. The mud mask tightening on her face was almost dry. Finish the movie, and then wash off the mask.

The movie couple embraced and managed to overlook the misunderstanding. Nina applauded the happy conclusion, but half listened for Ellie's voice. Whom was she talking to? Outside of Justin, she wasn't dating anyone else. Then the image of her and Daniel waving at them from shore, showing raucous high spirits came to mind. If she were talking to Daniel, she could ask about how Tony felt about her.

The immediacy of getting in contact with Tony had faded with Ellie's calamity. Her fingers touched the glass pendant, cool against her skin. No more, she rolled out of her prone position to hit the floor with a jolt. Thank goodness for carpet, hardwood floors would have hurt. Standing, she headed for the back bedroom yelling, "Wait, don't hang up."

Ellie stepped out of the bedroom, patting her face with a towel. "What are you yelling about?" The absence of her facial mask meant she had already hung up.

The question made Nina feel stupid. The request was something a middle school girl would stoop to as opposed to a grown, mature, self-confident woman. "Um, I was wondering if you wanted to see the rest of the movie."

Finished with the towel, she draped it around her neck. "No, I think I need to get into work early since I'll need to talk to HR about time off." She turned to go back to the bedroom, and made a half turned, remembering something else. "Oh, Daniel is coming by to see me tomorrow, here, if you don't mind."

"Of course, I don't mind." It would be good for her friend to get her mind off Mr. Biggs and the destruction of her home. She wanted to ask if he'd bring his hot friend with him, but didn't. She touched the pendant instead. It was an antique necklace and loaded with sentimental value. No man would have tossed it to a random woman.

Ellie gave her a brief hug before she retired. Nina picked up their dishes from their nachos fiesta. Long hours on the treadmill loomed ahead, resulting from the comfort food weekend. No problem, she could do it. A click of the remote sent the ecstatic couple frozen in each other's arms back to happy ending land.

Once in bed, her mind turned again to doubting if she would see Tony again. Fluffing up her already full feather pillow, she tried to find a comfortable spot to lay her head. There didn't seem to be any. Her neck bothered her too. Her fingers found the stiff neck muscle and massaged it. Stress was all it was. It had been a stress-provoking weekend, but it wasn't all bad stress.

Major work awaited her on the morrow. She had left a great deal undone at the main store. As for Tony, she considered herself good at reading people, the reason why she seldom had second dates. For the most part, she didn't like what she saw. Tony was sincere and not just playing her. Besides, she rationalized men didn't vanish until after they slept with you. Maybe she'd dream of Tony, but she didn't. Instead, she dreamed of Helen.

Nina walked down the familiar street with the intention of buying crystallized ginger at the spice shop when Helen appeared. She motioned her over with a too-bright smile.

The woman latched onto her when she was close enough. "Good, good, I have been waiting for you. There's been a mistake."

"A mistake," she repeated the words, not liking the sound of them. "What do you mean a mistake?"

The woman forced out a trilling laugh. "So silly, I believe the psychic phone lines got crossed. That Antonius fellow is not your soul mate. Nope, not for you." She patted Nina's arm with one hand while the other kept a firm grip as if she might make a break for it, a possibility with Nina not caring for what Helene was saying. Nina was quite content with the idea of Tony being her soul mate—more than content.

"Who should be my soul mate then?"

Helen patted her arm again. "So glad you asked. You've already met him. He adores you. He is waiting to hear from you this very minute."

"Who?" She pushed the word out through gritted teeth. If it were someone glorious, Helen should have told her straight out the first time.

The slender woman beamed at her, although the expression didn't reach her eyes. They had a desperate look to them. "Gavin."

"Gavin?" Her voice sounded shrill to her own ears. "Are you kidding me? The doofus who plastered me against my own car in a crowded public parking lot, trying to force himself on me?"

"True, his methods could use some polish." Helen's eyes held hers. "But he is your soul mate."

Nina shook off the woman's hands. "No thanks. I know my own heart and soul. I've already picked out my soul mate."

She walked away from the woman. Why she had ever believed her for her to talk nonsense now? She'd shown her Tony in the small globe. Did she or did I imagine him? Was my subconscious revealing the man most suited to me? Interesting concept, then my dreams segued into a hoard of glass and polystyrene pigs led by a very muscular Mr. Biggs chasing Justin.

Chapter Fourteen

N INA ARRIVED PROMPTLY at eight, beating the sales associates into the office, but not her secretary, Eugenia. The woman smiled at her as she started the first pot of coffee of the day. "Good Morning. It must have been an excellent holiday weekend."

The words gave her pause. Having Ellie's home trashed was less than desirable, but many good things came from the weekend. The image of Tony kissing her hands in the boat was one of them. A leftover memory of her telling the fortuneteller she'd pick out her own soul mate almost made her giggle, but she suppressed it.

"I guess I did have a good weekend. Made some difficult decisions. I'm putting my house on the market, and I'm considering trading in my car for something sportier."

"Woo-hoo," Eugenia exclaimed, surprising both of them. "I don't know what happened over the weekend, but you are too young to be living so old. Even with the twenty plus years, I have on you, I still act younger than you in regards to some things."

Nina sucked in her lips, but the woman was right. "I walk past your sunny yellow convertible every day. I imagine you have a boy toy to go with it."

"Goodness, have you extended your work into investigation? I thought David was my little secret." A contented look crossed her face as she reached for her labeled coffee cup. A few years ago, Eugenia made ceramic cups for everyone with their names emblazoned on them with her distinctive handwriting. She filled her cup, then filled Nina's, adding a dollop of hazelnut flavored creamer.

Accepting the cup, she took a sip and sighed in satisfaction. "This is so good. Who's David?"

Eugenia carried her cup to her desk, then sat down on her rolling chair with her usual grace, keeping her back straight and crossing her ankles in a demure fashion. "He's my younger boyfriend. He's only fifty-six. You should consider a younger man."

Really? A younger man? No, thank you. "I think I'm okay with men closer to my age." She cradled her coffee cup in her hand, heading for her office.

"I meant just a man, not necessarily younger," Eugenia called after her.

Nina closed her door and rested her back against it. At least no one else was in the place yet. She wasn't sure if she wanted Eugenia to take such an interest in her life. The woman devoted herself to work, and the result was she considered Nina not only her boss but also a proxy daughter in the bargain.

The morning flew by. She was able to make connections with all the people who left early for a holiday weekend. Her desk intercom chirped with Eugenia happily calling out a Mr. Dante was there to see her. Why it would make her so happy puzzled Nina.

Still, she had to give the rep credit. He tried several times to see her. The catalog was impressive. Did his consistent efforts mean no one else was buying Allegro suits, or he was a master sales representative? "Send him in."

She fingered the glass pendant while looking expectantly at the door. Most suit salesmen were older. Younger men failed to see the value of a suit in the United States. Not so in Europe though. A man in a well-tailored suit could practically have the woman of his choice and several of the men too. For some reason, they didn't use it as a company slogan.

Ironically, when the man walked through her door, she looked at the suit. A suit salesman served as his own walking billboard. She'd turned away more than one sales rep who showed up in an ill-fitting or rumpled looking suit. This was a nice suit, the body underneath was top notch too. The fabric weight indicated quality while still suitable for summer wear. The excellent drape of the fabric and the pants broke exactly right across the shoes. The color combination of the suit, shirt, and tie popped. She could imagine the combination on a mannequin in their showroom. Finally, her eyes reached a wide smile, flashing plenty of white teeth.

Oh my God! Here she was, evaluating the suit, and—her eyes met his. *Tony?*

"Tony," she said his name, but still looked surprised. "Um, I was waiting on a Mr. Dante, not that I'm not glad to see you."

He stepped completely into the office and closed the door. "Nina," he said her name in almost a caress as he approached her desk.

She pushed up from her desk and met him halfway. Did he open his arms? She couldn't remember. All she knew was she in his arms, kissing him. Her fingers combed through his close-cut hair. He pulled back enough for her to say. "I missed you so much."

His eyes twinkled. "Not as much as I missed you. I kicked myself for not getting your number. It was entirely my fault. You were so much like a dream come true. All weekend, I wondered if I could wait outside your gated community without the police being called."

Her lips met his for a short, sweet kiss reassuring her he was there in her office. "You aren't leaving without my number this time."

His sexy laugh warmed her, as did his smile, his arms, his lips, probably everything about him. Tony tightened his embrace, bringing their bodies flush as he lowered his lips for a kiss. The office door swung open just as he placed his lips on hers.

Eugenia's voice cut into the romantic atmosphere. "I wondered if Mr. Dante would like some—oh, I see you're taking my advice." The door shuts.

Mr. Dante. She took a step back. Maybe he wasn't Antonius Dunn. Perhaps Helen was right. What if he wasn't her soul mate? Her heart dropped. She didn't want anyone else, especially Gavin. "You are Mr. Dante, the man who was trying to see me the last two weeks and left me the excellent Sumatran blend?"

"Guilty as charged." He took a step back, aware something had changed.

Nina's lips twisted to one side. "Is it possible you attempted to romance me to gain a favorable attitude toward Allegro suits?" She moved, using the desk as a barrier, but did not sit.

His mouth fell open. "Are you frigging kidding me? I don't need your business. I don't resort to those types of tricks. I wouldn't do business with you now if you begged me. I wanted you, Nina, as a hot-blooded woman. Apparently, all I am to you is business. I saw the way you looked at me when I came in. Do all the sales rep offer sexual favors?"

Sexual favors. He thought she expected sexual favors from the sales representatives. Was she such a dried up prune she had to buy men's attention? There had to be steam coming out of her ears as her blood boiled. "I was looking at your suit. That's what I do. I wouldn't have you if you were the last man on earth."

Tony pivoted on one foot, stalked out the door, and slammed it. The door vibrated due to the force.

Eugenia crept in to find Nina leaning over her to-do list, allowing fat tears to hit it, blurring the ink.

"Practically a lightning storm in here with the two of you going at it. Surprised the place didn't burn down. So who is that man really? By the way, I never noticed you greeting the other sales reps quite so enthusiastically."

Eugenia stood behind Nina, rubbing smooth circles on her back. It was rather soothing. "Tony Dante is a pig-headed ass."

"He's a man so that sounds about right. You don't treat other men like that." She continued to rub Nina's back. "What is different about him?"

Nina attempted to clear her throat of the lingering thickness. She had an image to project as a competent boss, not some weepy female. This wasn't professional at all. The words slipped out before she considered them. "He's the only man I'll ever feel that way about, and yet, I accused him of romancing me to seal a deal."

One of Eugenia's hands, stopping rubbing her back, long enough to squeeze her shoulder in acknowledgment. "Oh, honey, the angry man who left here was not guilty of trying to sell suits." Eugenia shook her head slowly. "Makes me wonder if you two might have met before?"

"We have, many times in fact. Even on the Fourth of July, but he never told me his last name was Dante. The last time I met him, his name was Dunn. Men don't change their names. Do they? What reason would they have to? He deceived me." That's why she was so angry, wasn't it? A few sales reps had sent her flowers, hoping to win her over. After all, she was a female. They assumed she would fall for a bouquet. They figured wrong since she never did business with either one.

The heeltaps of Eugenia's pumps indicated she was on the move. Nina looked up to find the efficient woman returning with a glass of water, she placed on the desk.

"Drink it. It will help." She pulled an armchair neared to Nina. "Okay, this has all the earmarks of one of those romantic comedies."

Putting the glass to her lips, she took a few sips, before putting it down. "I am not laughing." The way she saw it, her last real chance at romance had just left the building in a huff. Her dream could be interpreted to mean something in the same vein. Still, she did not want Gavin. The only man she wanted appeared not to be talking to her.

Her secretary rested an elbow on her desk and cradled her chin in her hand. It was her thinking pose. Nina had seen it enough to recognize. Eugenia excelled at figuring at conundrums due to being a hardcore mystery buff. Her head came up and a light flickered in her eyes. "Did you mention your last names, the many times you met?"

Last name, did she ever mention it? The earlier meetings, they did have were little more than exchanging half dozen words. Names never came into play. She knew his name only because it was on his resume. Apparently, he didn't go by Antonius anymore. He did mention that, but never his last name, which explained his side. When they met on the Fourth, it had a dreamlike quality as if they were living out a scene already written for them. Ironically, they never formally introduced themselves.

"No, I don't think I did mention my last name. Friday's meeting was very untraditional. We didn't share names because we knew each other's first names already." Her voice softened as she consider how right everything was a few days ago, just the opposite of now.

Nina sighed and leaned back in her chair. Talk about behaving in an unprofessional manner. Her mother would laugh and say her Italian heritage was showing, but such displays were not good for business. "I guess I can't blame him not knowing my name, especially since I have N. Bradley on everything, but it doesn't explain his last name."

Tapping a lacquered nail against the desk, Eugenia smiled. "I think I have it. Men can change their names too. When he was investigating his heritage and found when his family emigrated, their name became wrong in the records. Most of the clerks could not spell foreign names well."

It sounded plausible, and she wanted it to be true. "The problem is Dunn and Dante sound nothing alike, except they both start with a D."

Clapping her hands together, her secretary said, "Wouldn't you change your name if it was Dunn and you worked in the world of fashion? Dun is a nondescript color or means to hound someone for payment. It would only cost two hundred dollars to change your name to Ziggy Stardust if you wanted to."

"There's some merit. I kept my name, Bradley, when I could have used my mother's maiden name, Alessandro, which has more panache." She said the words aloud, thinking how much she needed an acceptable reason for Tony's behavior. Eugenia held up her index finger.

"You love your father and are proud to carry his name, but what if your dad did something terrible, shamed and humiliated the family, for instance. Wouldn't you be tempted to drop his name to show he was dead to you?" She ended her words with a dramatic slashing gesture of her hand.

Her theatrics caused an unexpected giggle. "You know me too well. Of course, I would. You've given me a great deal to think about. I should call and apologize. Let me see if I can find his number among all these messages." She reached to pull the desk phone closer to her, but Eugenia reached to cover her hand, stopping her.

"Wait. Take some advice from a woman a little wiser and older. You may have wondered why I never married. It wasn't because I never wanted to. I just didn't play my hand well enough. Right now, your man is angry-hot."

Nina wanted to argue the part about him being her man, but she didn't.

"He's gone off somewhere to lick his wounds. Give him time to think about how much you mean to him."

She wanted to point out it might be a problem, especially if she didn't mean much to him. Her fingers smoothed over the glass pendant, lifting it and running her thumb over the backside. She caught Eugenia's interested gaze.

She started to unhook the necklace to allow her secretary to see it closer but decided against it. Tony put it around her neck. Though superstitious, she feared taking it off might sever the tenuous bond between the two of them. Holding it up, it allowed a better view for Eugenia.

"Tony gave it to me Friday. It's a family heirloom his great grandfather, a glass blower, made it for his great grandmother as a courting gift. She never took it off. It's supposed to be given to your soul mate, and Tony gave it to me." She said the words with a sense of wonder. Did this occur only forty-eight hours ago?

Eugenia's index finger made a thorough sweep underneath each eye as she sniffed. "Goodness, I think that is going to make me cry. Well, apparently my help isn't needed here. Looks like fate has the two of you in her hands."

Fate. She wasn't so sure she trusted her. Consider the many times she and Tony could have met, or briefly met, but did not connect. Fate was slacking on her job. A hurried search of her desk unearthed the message Tony sent with the coffee. His business card was with it, as she knew it would be.

Glancing at the door, she hoped her secretary wouldn't catch her in the act of doing the thing she warned against doing. Punching in the numbers, she wondered what she would say. Of course, she should apologize, but her actions made their holiday interlude meaningless if she thought he was a shyster, a scam artist.

His voice came on the line, calm and professional. "Tony Dante, how can I help you?"

She placed the handset quietly back on the base, shutting off the connection. Hanging up on the man wasn't helpful, either. No doubt, he had her number on caller ID. What could she do? With any luck, during the day a lightning flash of romantic brilliance would hit. She doubted it would happen, but it was better than moping all day, which is what she did more or less.

Her associates avoided her. No one asking questions after a long weekend was peculiar. She suspected Eugenia's hand in the fact everyone left her alone. When she walked out on the sales floor, she garnered a few curious, questioning, and interested glances, especially from the female sales rep. Then it hit her, everyone may have heard their argument. If not the argument, they couldn't have missed a steamed Tony slamming through the building. Women would definitely notice him, which explained their curiosity. Probably wondering why she would argue with such a fine specimen. Made her wonder too, so, she slunk back to her office. Quitting time could not come soon enough.

Chapter Fifteen

NINA ACCUSED HIM of playing up to her to make a sale! His anger must have risen off him in visible waves, which deflected people out of his way as strode through the mall. Really, did she think so little of his merchandise he would have to make himself into some type of gigolo to move it? The way she looked at him earlier indicated she approved of the merchandise, very much so. A corner of his lips quirked up when she said she was looking at the suit. She could have been, but her glance felt similar to fingers running up his body instead of her eyes.

No way was Nina Bradley indifferent to him. The thought intrigued him, slowing his retreat from the mall. Yes, no way around it, leaving the scene to rethink strategy equaled a retreat, no matter how he'd like to think otherwise. Past time to consider his options over a cup of java, although coffee may have started the entire meltdown. The secretary mentioned his name when she almost asked him if he wanted coffee, which explained Nina's reaction when she discovered he was Mr. Dante.

He never hid his name, and the secretary had warned Nina a Mr. Dante was on his way. At the time, he thought it was cute, but he never thought she was serious. No wonder she went ballistic. She thought he played her for a fool by not mentioning his name. When she called him Tony the other day, he thought she knew it, all of it.

He stopped at a coffee stand, putting down his briefcase and keys, and reached for his wallet to pay the barista. Shouldering his briefcase and picking up his coffee, he headed for the car and solitude.

"Hey, man, you forgot your keys."

Tony turned slightly at the words to notice the grinning barista shaking his car keys. He walked back to take his keys from the multi-tattooed male.

"Thanks," he growled the word, which translated in his mind, thanks for showing everyone what I fool I am.

"Some babe got you by the short hairs, huh?" The male, barely old enough to be out of school, made the casual observation.

The worse part about it was he called it right. Tony grunted in response, unwilling to get into a discussion of women with a male half his age. He nodded and resumed his walk. Romance was easy for kids that age. They didn't expect much and hadn't acquired too much baggage. They easily hooked up and often disconnected with hardly a thought. Of course, they were clueless how hard things would get.

The pool of appropriate women grew smaller with each year. Smart men held onto the truly remarkable women. Those few who entered the dating scene due to divorce or spousal death vanished in mere months. This only left the Sheilas of the world. His shoulders scrunched up at the thought. How could he convince Nina of his real intent? Then again, he wasn't the one at fault.

Unlocking his car, he slid into the scorching car, glad for the pants that shielded his skin from the leather seats frying his legs. He twisted the key to start the car and promptly turned the air conditioning to the max and rolled down the windows to allow the heat to escape. Not that it would do too much immediately. He discovered leather seats, especially black ones held onto the heat. His phone rang, the ID shows *Prestige Suits*, which meant it could be Nina or the secretary informing him he'd no longer be welcome on the premises.

"Tony Dante. How can I help you?"

There was a moment of silence, before the phone disconnected, indicating it had to be Nina. What did that mean? No threat, no ultimatum, and no apology? Even with almost forty years on earth, he was no closer to understanding women than when he first became aware of females at the grand age of four. In preschool, Rita Mae Taylor slugged him. His mother told him it meant she liked him, but he was sure it meant the opposite. His belief any attention from women indicated interest gave him a tiny spark of hope, though.

The Rita Maes felt like slugging a man while the Sheilas took what they could. He could understand that, but the very complex, Nina baffled him. She called only to hang up. As a business executive, she might be interested in the suits. She already demonstrated she was very interested in him as a man. Why the hang-up call?

He knew. A chuckle broke free when he realized she was almost as stubborn as he was. When she realized she was in the wrong, she knew she had to apologize if only for professional reasons. As a driven, proud woman, he bet she could count on one hand the times she'd apologized. The kind thing would be to call her to smooth over the situation. His open hand ran over his chin. He'd let her squirm. Nina had not only insulted his honor after he gave her his family heirloom, but she also insulted his suits, inferring he'd have to romance her to get her to buy.

Throughout the day, Tony fought the desire to call Nina. Even harder was when she called him a second time, at least he thought it was her. He had finished a successful call and some paperwork when the phone rang. The number was the same. He let it go to voice mail. He made himself wait an entire minute before listening. Playing it back, he heard her sweet voice. It quivered with uncertainty. She must hate putting her apology on voice mail. Too bad, he didn't answer. He played it again.

"Tony, I should say Tony Dante. I'm sorry for my behavior. My only defense is often some men believe a woman in the business of men's suit is just a figurehead. I'm not. All the same," her voice caught, "what I said was wrong. If you can overlook it, I would be more than happy to examine your merchandise. Nina Bradley."

She was willing to examine his suits. There was no mention of him or them, or anything else. It was not what he wanted. It would be easy enough to call the secretary and set up another appointment. He wanted something more personal. Before, the suit deal had loomed large in his agenda, but not so much anymore. There would be other companies and other buyers he could interest. The only deal he wanted to close involved Nina and him, an exclusive contract.

The phone burbled. Anxious and hoping it was Nina for a second apology or maybe to withdraw her original apology, he tapped his thumb on the send button, without taking the time to look at the ID. It didn't matter as long as it was hers. The word 'private' flashed on the phone, which meant it could possibly be her since his phone had been doing that a lot lately. He injected as much warmth and sex appeal as he could into his voice.

"Hello, I'm so pleased you called me."

Daniel's voice cackled at the other end. "You sly dog, I never knew you cared."

He should have known better than to expect Nina to call again. "Yeah, you're not who I expected."

He laughed again and added, "Oh really? Well, you might change your mind once you hear the facts. Ellie's house was trashed over the weekend by an ex-boyfriend who also killed her cat."

Why Daniel thought this would change his mind puzzled him.

"That sucks." It might explain Nina's quick jump to the worst conclusion attitude.

"Yes, it does." Danny happily agreed. "Ellie deserves so much better than scum like that. I bought her a kitten to replace the dead one."

Tony shot his free hand through his hair. "I don't know. She might have wanted to pick out her own replacement cat."

"Oh." Dejection filled the one small word.

He did it again, crushed his buddy's happiness. He criticized him when he tried to be a swinging bachelor, now he found fault with his attempts to be a nice guy. "What do I know about women? I bet she'll love it."

Daniel readily agreed. "You don't know much about women. I'm taking the kitten over to Ellie tonight. Since she's staying with Nina, I thought you might like to go with me. Nudge, nudge, wink, wink."

The desire to argue the point about not knowing much about women stuck in his throat, but he had started it. He'd see Nina in the company of his friend. It was obvious she'd see through it, but currently it was all he had.

"Good. Be glad to go. What time?" He held the phone to his ear, contemplating a peace offering. A small voice reminded him he was right. Did he want to be right and alone or happy? Happy sounded preferable, which was why he ended up holding a kitten in a box the entire way to Nina's house.

Oscar, the name Daniel picked out for it, showed anxiety while traveling. Nerves caused him to stick his needle sharp claws into Tony's hands. Could be Oscar had homicidal tendencies and hoped to destroy a small part of him, one scratch at a time. His hands felt somewhat numb so it must be working.

They hadn't driven more than a mile when Oscar escaped from his cardboard box and fought all efforts to put him back in. Daniel's uncontrolled laughter exacerbated his aggravation. He settled the wayward feline in his lap. The orange striped kitten had failed the cute test. He only hoped Ellie would overlook the feline's muddled bloodlines and out of proportion features. His head and feet belonged to a much larger cat.

Because Daniel insisted on driving, his car avoided the cat hair. Not so much his clothes, but they were washable. The clumps of cat hair on his linen trousers made him wish he'd taken the time to change. He wanted to make a good impression on Nina. Oh, no it didn't, but it had. A warm, spreading patch of wetness covered his inner thigh. Not a good place for cat urine when it could be mistaken for something else.

"Daniel, your cat wet on me." He held it away from him in distaste. The little monster sported a pleased smile.

"Calm down, we're almost there." He pulled into the gated entry, up to the keypad, and quickly entered the number. "Besides, he's a kitten. He isn't supposed to be housetrained yet."

"You could have mentioned it." He held onto the miscreant, knowing if he let go they might lose him. Oscar mimicked Houdini with his escape artistry.

Daniel slowly drove down the streets, peering at the ornate signs. "We're looking for 657 Horatio Hornblower Walk."

"Horatio Hornblower was a literary character. Will we eventually turn onto Jay Gatsby Boulevard?" The fictional character names, but probably came from an Internet search. It puzzled him why Nina lived here.

Daniel pulled into the drive, parked the car, and reached for the cat. "I want to carry little Oscar in. You can tote the cat box and food."

He didn't really want to go in. He was a mess from his scratched hands to reeking of cat urine. Most people wouldn't let him in.

Maybe Nina would allow him to sponge off his pants in the bathroom at least.

Ellie threw open the front door as if expecting Daniel. He'd give the man credit. He must have alerted her he had a surprise. It would build a sense of anticipation. He hoped the actual presence of Oscar didn't destroy too much.

Ellie squealed. She picked up the feline delinquent and nuzzled it. Daniel got a kiss on his cheek for his efforts, which appeared to please him by his goofy expression. Nina appeared and ushered them all in the door. She took one look at him and said, "What happened to you?"

"Cat," he angled his head in Oscar's direction since his hands were full.

Her eyes followed the happy couple and their feline. "Keep the cat on the screened-in porch. I am trying to sell this place, I don't need it to smell like..." she turned to look at him and the spot on his pants, "... you."

Great. Did she have to smile when she said '*you*'? "I think I can sponge it off."

She shook her head in disagreement. "Cat urine is one of the worst. The smell stays forever if you don't treat it immediately."

Forever. He liked these pants. Depositing the litter box and food on the couch, he waited for her instructions.

Her eyes went to the spot again. "You're going to have to take your pants off. There are no two ways about it.

Daniel walked in the living room to gather up the cat supplies while she was speaking and raised one eyebrow. Nina didn't notice him, which was just as well.

"The only problem is I didn't bring any extra clothes because I didn't expect this to happen." It was hard to be serious with only half a suit on.

"Wait here." Nina disappeared from view, only to return clutching a long section of red and black material. She shook it out revealing an ornate Japanese kimono. "My cousin Julian bought this for his girlfriend when he was stationed in Japan. She had dumped him before he returned, and I received it by default. Found out later it was a man's kimono, which would not have pleased the girlfriend, but it works for you."

She wanted him to put on a kimono. Men sporting cat hair and urine didn't have much dignity left. "Okay," he agreed and held his hand out for the robe.

She pointed to the room behind her. "You can change in my room. There is a bathroom attached if you need it."

The open door revealed a cherry bedroom suite with a rice planter bed. She trusted him. Her gesture didn't go unnoticed. Could be it was her way of apologizing. Slipping off his shoes, he started to undress while taking inventory of the room. There was no evidence of men's clothes, shoes, or even male toiletries on the dresser. Personal touches existed throughout the room, except for a small framed picture of a younger Nina and an elderly woman. Most likely, this was a photo of her beloved Nona Caprice.

He left his jacket on the bed, which would have been bulky under the kimono, not to mention hot. He pulled off his socks thinking they might look foolish too. He tightened the tie around his waist, grimacing the material ending well above his ankles. A castoff kimono didn't radiate confident male, but he still had the bottle of *Five Roses* Italian wine in the car.

Combined voices came from the back of the house as he opened the bedroom door. It would give him time to get the wine while they oohed and ahhed over the antics of the furball. After Nina joking about the neighborhood being a virtual ghost town, he was surprised to see two older women power walking and a man walking his schnauzer along the sidewalk. The three of them gave him a methodical once over. Trying to ignore his awkwardness, he waved at the gawkers.

The three of them looked away quickly, perhaps embarrassed at being caught staring. It only took a couple of feet and a few seconds to grab the bottle of wine. With the wine bottle tucked under his arm, he headed back to the house, but the door he had left partially open mocked him with its closed state. Did it close on its own or did Nina push it shut? Multiple stabs on the doorbell yielded no results.

A father followed two children driving motorized child-size cars, which careened across carefully groomed lawns. A woman followed, pushing a screened stroller with a dog in it. She may or may not have been the mother of the two previous children, considering the dog in the stroller. The mother looked at him curiously, he held up his hand in greeting once again. It would be nice to get inside the house and out of public view.

The door swung open. "There you are. Get in here." Nina tugged on his sleeve.

"Gladly." He stepped into the house. "I rang the bell, but no one came."

"Really?" She leaned out the open door and pushed the buzzer. "No sound. It doesn't work. Who knows how long it hasn't."

He grinned. "I thought you were just ignoring me and making me stand outside in this kimono was some type of punishment." He wiggled his eyebrows to try to make light of the moment.

"Good heavens, no. I have to live here until I sell this place. Who knows? Strange men in inappropriate dress might be subject to a fine. Until now, I never did anything worthy of my neighbors' attention." She nodded to the bottle under his arm. "For me?"

"Yes," He presented the bottle with a flourish. "I thought you would appreciate a nice Italian rosé-style wine."

She reached for the wine, her fingers brushing his. For a brief moment, they both held onto the bottle, their eyes meeting. Surely, she felt the same pull.

Her lips parted. She sighed heavily. "Is there any chance we can start over? You could pretend I didn't react like an over emotional female today."

He pretended to consider. "Well, I might be willing to cut you a deal." His wink caused her lips to curve upward.

Her fingers caressed his before she took the bottle. "Let's hear this deal." She carried the wine to the kitchen and placed it in the freezer to speed up the chilling.

Following her gave him an unobstructed view of her sexy walk. His soul mate, no way was he letting her go. She spun around and caught him staring. Caught in the act, he could only shrug. "Guilty," he admitted, "of admiring beauty."

"Come here." She crooked her index finger in a beckoning gesture.

He sauntered up to her, unsure what would happen next. When she wrapped her arms around him, he saw it as an excellent indication of reconciliation. Their lips met, and it felt like something shifted inside him. He opened his eyes to observe her shocked expression. "Did you feel it?"

"I did. What was it?" There was a sense of wonder in her voice.

Tony didn't know how to put his knowing into words, but he would try. "I think it is what happens when two soul mates meet and everything falls into place."

"Oh, is that all." Her voice grew husky. "Now about the deal," she reminded him, running her fingers through his hair.

"I haven't forgotten. First, we'll save my pants, and then, when the wine is chilled, we can discuss our plans. I foresee you living in a community with a lot less silly rules." He dropped soft kisses on her hair as he predicted possibilities.

Nina's laugh rang out throaty and low, before she asked, "Is there any chance I'll meet my soul mate?"

Hugging her tight, he murmured the words into her hair. "You already have, seven times, well more than seven."

Epilogue

HELEN AND GAVIN peered into a large crystal ball featuring the embracing Tony and Nina. The woman shook her head in disgust. "Did you hear him using my lines? No respect."

Gavin gave the woman an irritated look. "Do you want to talk about respect? How come I always have to be the creepy boyfriend who pushes the woman into her soul mate's arms?"

Helen's mouth twisted into a wry expression. "Some women need convincing that they are lovable and a soul mate is waiting. Nina was one of them. Look at how long I've been trying to get those two together."

Gavin reached for two wine glasses and poured champagne into them. He offered one glass to Helen and held the other one up. "To another successful pairing." The crystalline sound of glasses clinking filled the silence.

Gavin took a large swallow. "Good stuff. Great job this time, Helen. I was afraid they wouldn't get together on the seventh chance."

She waved one hand airily. "Oh, I just made that number up to give her a sense of urgency. To wake her up some. I would have kept throwing those two together even in their sixties."

"In their sixties?" Gavin's mouth fell open for a few seconds.

Helen puts a finger under his chin and pushed it close. "Didn't you ever wonder why those lifelong bachelors and spinsters get married in their golden years? Those are my severe cases. These two weren't too bad, considering."

THE END

The Love Talisman

Book Two of The Soul Mate Series

December 2016

MR. BIGG'S HOARSE meow served as an alarm clock, reminding her she needed to get up and feed her pet. Ellie rolled over, taking her pillow with her and covering her face. Her cat wouldn't hesitate to bat her face to drive his point home. He had in the past. Besides, her head throbbed like tiny dancers doing an early morning rendition of Riverdance inside her head.

Underneath the covering of her pillow, she took personal inventory. Her leg moved across the mattress. Alone, unless she counted one irritated cat. Head hurt and her tongue felt like cotton. Both she contributed to the half dozen cosmopolitans she made herself last night. At least, she drank at home and not at some dubious bar, making a fool of herself. She'd tried to interest in Nina in going out with her, but her friend was all work and seldom had time for socializing after taking the regional manager job. Sometimes it seemed like no one had time for her, especially Justin.

Technically, she referred to Justin as her boyfriend, but Nina called him a series of names from selfish S.O. B. to bad decision. Her friend wasn't shy about sharing her opinion.

Her bent finger rubbed her sore eye. No doubt, it would be both puffy and bloodshot. Liquor and self-pity didn't make a good combination.

Mr. Biggs head butted her pillow and raised the volume of his complaints. She should get up. No reason for her to stay in bed. The world hadn't ended because her sweetie called up at the last minute telling her why he couldn't swing by for the gourmet dinner she made. Cooking shows were her addiction. Recipes didn't cost anything, even though the ingredients did. They didn't break, and they never left snarky messages on social media.

Last night wasn't the first time he stood her up. Her lips twisted as she tried to remember how many times she'd been disappointed in their relationship. Her fingers went up under the sheet as she counted. Three if you counted the work excuse. Once he claimed to be sick, that would be four. When he stood her up the first time, she made the mistake of telling Nina.

Her best friend ranted so long and hard you'd think she was the one stood up. Her constant refrain to dump him grated on Ellie's nerves. That sealed her decision not to mention that all wasn't well. On the flip side, at least she had someone.

The pillow depressed flattening across her face as her kitty kneaded it in preparation for laying down. "Okay. You win." She shoved the pillow aside and blinked in the bright light. Odd, did she leave the light on too? A half roll revealed the curtains were open. The morning light flooded the room. Her lips twisted to one side as she considered the meaning of this unexpected development. *What day was it?*

Justin only came over on the weeknights. Nina used this idiosyncrasy has proof he was married or involved with someone else. Didn't make much sense to her because a wife would object any night that her husband wasn't at home. Justin never stayed the night, but she put that down to commitment issues. Many men were like that or at least the ones she'd met.

She did the payroll yesterday, so checks could go out today, which meant it was Friday. The revelation had her jackknifing into position. *Oh my God, work. Not only should she be at work, but also today was payday.* Generally, she enjoyed passing out paychecks to the rugged construction workers who staffed the various crews. It made her feel like Lady Bountiful. She was some benevolent goddess passing out favors to muscle bound men with bicep tattoos.

Unfortunately, the men didn't recognize her as such. Most called her kid, little sister, or even peanut due to her lack of height. She served more as a mascot than an accounting goddess. Little sister or goddess, the men would be peeved if she didn't get their paychecks to them in a timely fashion. A sharp trio of knocks set her into motion.

"Great. Now what." She half-hopped, half ran to the front door trying not to trip over Mr. Bigg, who twined between the legs. He probably felt his needs came first since he started his wake-up call much earlier. Who could be knocking on her door? Well, she knew who it wasn't. Justin.

Using the footstool, she kept by the door, she slid in front of the door before she hopped onto it. Why locksmiths insisted on putting peepholes so high always baffled her. A strapping six-foot man probably never peered out the door before swinging it open. Little old ladies, children, and those in the height-challenged department did, which meant the hole could be about five inches lower to accommodate.

Kelley, her landlord, stood on the landing with her rubber glove clad hands perched on her hips. Instead of knocking again, she spoke instead. "I know you're behind the door. Open up."

The duplex sold her on its spaciousness and low price. The contract didn't specify that the proprietor would not only keep the unit up to snuff, but would use her tough love skills on the occupant too. Might as well open the door, it would be more like holding a tornado back otherwise. Reluctantly, she swung the door open.

Kelley gave her the once over, starting at the bottom of her Hello Kitty pajamas, working her way up to her Medusa locks. A comment on her childlike sleepwear she expected, but it wasn't what she got.

"You look like shit. Should I assume you aren't going to work? I could hear Mr. Biggs crying his heart out and for a second, I thought something happened to you." One of her rubber gloved cover hands went to her chest demonstrating her dismay.

Ah, yes, an explanation of sorts was customary. *Well, I got stinking drunk because I was stood up again. I do have plenty of roasted lamb if you'd like some.* She sucked in her lips, holding in that excuse. Her mind lighted on the fact, Kelley could hear Mr. Biggs meowing. What else did she hear? Ellie squeezed her eyes shut not wanting to consider the various things she didn't want to be heard. Some things should stay private. "Hard time getting started." She gripped the door harder, realizing she was wasting time talking when she should be racing off to work.

"I see." She gave a sage nod of her head and pivoted to go.

Ellie almost had the door closed before Kelley called back. "He's not good enough for you."

She closed the door without answering. Even her landlady felt the need to comment on her love life. Mr. Biggs plopped down by the kitchen entrance and meowed plaintively several times. A non-cat person would think he was merely hungry. She knew better. She got the coffee maker going before she finished listening to her feline dress down. "I know you don't like him, either. I'll admit he's not good with cats."

Her cat gave a definite meow. The cat agreed. Of course, he did. A juicy exhale of the pop-top of his cat food causes an impatient tail switch. In too much of a hurry to scrape the food out, she placed the can on the floor. Her fluffy Himalayan had cast a disdainful look at the can before he picked at the food.

Ellie rolled her eyes. Mr. Biggs could outdo any diva, feline or human. He had definite preferences, and Justin wasn't one of them. "I know you don't like him," she started as she pushed the bread into the toaster. "It isn't easy to meet men over a certain age. The majority of them are married or in a relationship by twenty-five. As for the rest," she sighed before finishing, "it's obvious why they aren't."

The image of Kelley listening while scrubbing her kitchen sink, which happened to be on the other side of the wall, stilled her explanation. Mr. Biggs stopped eating and looked up at the interruption.

Um, yeah, she usually talked as he ate. It made her feel less lonely and apparently, he expected it. The coffee gurgled to a stop, and the toast popped up. *Breakfast of Champions or time-stressed accountants.* Coffee in one hand and toast in the other she made her way to the bedroom.

As she dressed and munched her way through breakfast, she glanced at her rumpled bed. How much did Kelley hear? Memories of her previous apartment with the loud talker underneath her made her cringe a little as she stepped into her flats. Often, she wore heels or even platforms to compensate for her height. Not today didn't have time. The clock, which hadn't gone off for some reason, showed she was already ninety minutes behind schedule. She'd have to drive to each construction site to hand-deliver the checks before she could even start today's work. "Thanks, Justin, you A-hole." Mr. Biggs strolled into the room adding his meow to the statement.

The drive to work, put her smack in rush hour traffic. Since the construction day, often started to dawn and sometimes before, she forgot so many other people went to work later. The glut of cars surrounding her along with the bevy of horns brought that fact home. A glance at her fellow drivers revealed a few on cell phones, another half dozen with a coffee cup to their lips. The man in the sports car next to her was shaving. The woman in front of her had her rear view mirror angled, which meant makeup. "People pay attention, and we'd get somewhere."

The yelling didn't help. The traffic crept along a little slower than a glacier moved. A side street beckoned. A flick of her blinker and she turned out of the mayhem. Her speed picked up as she bumped along the county road. Every now and then, her knowledge of alternative routes paid off. She wouldn't have ever ventured down this way, if her company hadn't built a church on it. Let all those other commuters simmer in the summer heat.

Her morning grumpiness wore away as she neared work. Justin not showing or making excuses at the last minute for why he couldn't come was becoming more and more common. The thought made her uncomfortable. She twisted up the radio volume and started singing along with a rock classic. It reminded her of high school, not that high school was that great of an experience. She spent most of her time assuring the teachers that she really was a student there, and not a middle school student sneaking into classes. Why would a middle school student want to do that? Better yet, why would she keep coming back?

The song ended with her belting out the chorus. The smooth voice DJ came on. "For those of you experiencing romantic problems today, this one is for you." The music started softly but gradually became loud enough for Ellie to recognize the words of a terse ballad about taking an arrow straight to her heart. Instead of falling in love, the arrow just hurt. Even her favorite radio station was against her.

"That's it. You're history." Her fingers punched scan, which enabled the radio to find the next strongest signal. Anything would better than the previous song. The scan stuttered over a couple of weak signals, settling on a woman speaking. "Do you ever wonder why you have never met your soul mate?"

Ellie sighed. Again. The scan would move on in a couple of seconds if she didn't touch it. She answered the radio voice. "Yes, I do." Couldn't talk it out with Mr. Biggs once aware her property owner might overhear.

"It could be your choice of dating material."

Wait a minute, shouldn't the scan move on. "Nina, is that you? Are you playing the world's most elaborate practical joke on me?"

Her right hand felt around the radio to see if any wires lead away from it. Her friend might be able to manage a feed into her radio system. Nothing. Although, it sounded exactly like what Nina would say. Her principal complaint was she dated men who didn't treat her well. Her response was that Nina didn't date at all. That wasn't entirely true, but it shut her friend up for a while.

The radio voice continued. "Do you long for a man to accept you as you are and not some knock-off copy of a celebrity?" Her eyes widened considering how a radio voice knew Justin always wanted to role-play with her assuming the role of a famous singer while he was the music producer. The wig she always had to wear made her head itch.

Being herself would be nice for a change. Going out and having other people fix meals would be nice, too. There was so much she wanted to do, but never mentioned it knowing Justin would shoot down her ideas. It was easier not to suggest things than face rejection.

"Yes, I do radio voice. Any suggestions?"

The voice continued, the accent more pronounced than before. "What you need is a romance aid."

Her eyebrows shot up at the word, romance. "Seriously. I'm sure that would be in four convenient payments of $19.95." The aid would consist of a miniscule vial of pheromone oil that smelt like sweaty gym socks. Not sure, how that attracted anyone.

Static filled the air as the radio searched for another station. *Now.*

The radio changes stations. The theme music of the old-timey gospel hour filled the car. Elle recognized it since her grandmother always listened to it. A gravel-voiced minister spoke. "Believe. You have to believe. There is no power without belief."

"Believe what?" Listen to her talk back to the radio. Was she in a current day version of *The Twilight Zone* where everyday devices offered advice. Worse yet, she not only talked back, but was actually starting to consider the random words as directions for living.

"Okay, radio spirits, or whatever you are. Tell me what I need?" The light turned green allowing her to shoot through it. Almost there, if karma, fate, or whatever possessed the radio could put some speed on. Static filled the speakers as the search progressed. A swell of big band music filled the car, reminding her of all the old black and white movies she watched with her grandmother. The actors and actresses were always so elegantly dressed. Even the not so perfect men left merely with a door close or a regretful glance. They never had to be a jerk about it.

A singer with a voice like a nightingale sang about someone to watch over her. A snort of disgust escaped her lips. "Really car radio. Is that the best you can do? I've never had anyone to watch over me, except for my grandparents."

Her hand brushed against her cheek to wipe away any telltale moisture that might have somehow appeared. She always got emotional when it came to her parents. She never talked about them. Ever. She made the mistake of mentioning them once to Elle. Her best friend couldn't understand parents who would drop off the children at the grandparents and disappear for all practical purposes. No tragic story about an accident taking both parents at the same time. Some of the other students lived with grandparents because their parents were deployed, in rehab, or prison. Hers just left her and her brother with her maternal grandparents. No lead up to it, no reasoning, just a promise to see them later, one they never made good on.

Stupid radio. She pulled into the parking lot and turned off the ignition. She took a couple of deep breaths to get herself together. She didn't need parents who didn't need her. Her grandmother assured her that her daughter and son-in-law were too immature to be parents. Of course, they must have realized this after she was ten and her brother eight. It wouldn't help thinking about it. It never did. Ellie slammed the car door, hoping she could close the subject of her abandonment just as easily.

Her boss stepped out of the door and tugged on his ball cap. Elle smiled at him. Harry was like a big, gruff bear. Make that a bearded, balding bear. That's what the ball cap was for. It allowed him to pretend there was more hair underneath beside the broad fringe at the rim of the cap. "Hey there, short stuff, I was starting to worry about you."

Short stuff again, didn't anyone remember her name? Her lips pulled up into a tired smile. "I had some problems this morning."

He held up one hand. "Say no more. You're here that's all that matter. Termite has already called about paychecks for his crew." The gurgle of the phone ringing through the door indicated someone else needed to comment on the lack of paychecks.

She pointed to the office. "I bet that's Lightbulb calling."

"Probably." Harry agreed with a nod. "Thought I'd meet you at the door with the checks." He held out a handful of envelopes to her. Her hand closed around them as she spoke.

"Are you sure they're all there?" Typically, she didn't question her boss. "Last time, Thor's check was missing, and it wasn't pleasant." The Nordic giant they hired recently bore a striking resemblance to the actor who play Thor. The resemblance stopped there since their version had no personality. He hardly talks and answered more in grunts with the occasional withering look.

Her boss laughed and slapped her on the shoulder. "No worries. I think he might be sweet on you. Go spread your payday magic. I know the men and Robby will be delighted to see you."

Robby, the only female carpenter, somehow escaped her boss' fondness for nicknames. All in all, short stuff wasn't too bad, considering he labeled one of the men ass dragger. The other employees just called his ass for short. Another unfavorable nickname was Turd for the plumber journeyman. Short Stuff sounded better and better.

"Okay." She waved the checks in her hand. "I'm out on delivery duty. I'll be back before lunch." She pivoted to leave, wondering if the car radio would offer any more romantic tips.

"Take lunch out," Harry yelled after her. "You look like you deserve a treat."

Author Notes

- If you enjoyed this book, please lend it to a friend.

- Write a review.

- Do you have an idea for a story or a character name? Love to hear it. I can be reached through my website at www.morgankwyatt.com

- Want to get free books, read excerpts before everyone else, receive special members only swag and giveaways? You need to be on the mailing list. Go over to my website and sign up. (I don't sell my mailing list and guard it as well as I do my chocolate.)

- Do you like humor with your suspense? Check out my new cozy mystery series that I wrote with my husband. Book one of *The Painted Lady Inn Mysteries* is **Murder Mansion.** We write under the combined name of M.K. Scott

- Love to meet you, check out my personal appearances on the website too.

- Can you do one more thing? Go out and have an amazing day.

Morgan K Wyatt